Your home
making the biggest mistake of his life
in believing you."

Corrie stiffened at the flash of steel under Lucas's lazy drawl.

"If Mr. Manning wants to invite me here, I can't see that it's any of your concern."

"Anything that affects the family concerns me. Especially a con artist trying to convince an old man she's his long-lost granddaughter."

"I've told the lawyers and Mr. Manning. Now I'll tell you. I don't want anything from him."

"No secret dreams of being the missing heiress, coming into all that lovely money?" He smiled slowly, his eyes intent on her face, as if he tried to see beneath the surface. "Then we have to make sure you enjoy your time here, don't we?"

Books by Marta Perry

Love Inspired

A Father's Promise #41
Since You've Been Gone #75
*Desperately Seeking Dad #91
*The Doctor Next Door #104
*Father Most Blessed #128
A Father's Place #153
†Hunter's Bride #172
†A Mother's Wish #185
†A Time To Forgive #193
†Promise Forever #209
Always in Her Heart #220
The Doctor's Christmas #232
True Devotion #241
**Hero in Her Heart #249
**Unlikely Hero #287
**Hero Dad #296
**Her Only Hero #313

*Hometown Heroes
†Caldwell Kin
**The Flanagans

Love Inspired Suspense

In the Enemy's Sights #19
Land's End #24
Tangled Memories #28

MARTA PERRY

has written everything from Sunday school curriculum to travel articles to magazine stories in twenty years of writing, but she feels she's found her home in the stories she writes for Love Inspired.

Marta lives in rural Pennsylvania, but she and her husband spend part of each year at their second home in South Carolina. When she's not writing, she's probably visiting her children and her beautiful grandchildren, traveling or relaxing with a good book.

MARTA PERRY
Tangled
MEMORIES

Steeple
Hill®

Published by Steeple Hill Books™

STEEPLE HILL BOOKS

Steeple
Hill®

ISBN-13: 978-0-373-87384-5
ISBN-10:   0-373-87384-0

TANGLED MEMORIES

www.SteepleHill.com

Printed in U.S.A.

You know me inside and out,
You know every bone in my body;
You know exactly how I was made, bit by bit,
how I was sculpted from nothing into something.
—*Psalms* 139:15

This story is dedicated to my grandson,
Bjoern Jacob Wulff, with much love from Grammy.
And, as always, to Brian.

ONE

For twenty-nine years, Corrie Grant had thought she'd never know who her father was. Now she knew, and no one would believe her.

No one, at this point, was represented by a pair of smooth, silver-haired attorneys with Southern drawls as thick as molasses. They looked about as expensive as this hotel suite, where she sank to the ankles in plush carpeting. The denim skirt and three-year-old sweater she usually wore for her monthly shopping trip had definitely not been right for this meeting. She hadn't known Cheyenne, Wyoming boasted a hotel suite like this.

She slid well-worn loafers under her chair and straightened her back. *You're as good as anyone,* her great-aunt's voice echoed in her mind, its independent Wyoming attitude strong. *Don't you let anyone intimidate you.*

"I've already told you everything I know about my parents." Her words stopped one of the lawyers—Courtland or Broadbent, she didn't know which—in mid-question. "I came here to meet Baxter Manning." Her grandfather. She tried out the phrase in her mind, not quite ready to say it aloud yet. "Where is he?"

"Now, Ms. Grant, surely you understand that we have

to ascertain the validity of your claim before involving Mr. Manning, don't you?"

Courtland or Broadbent had the smooth Southern courtesy down pat. He'd just managed to imply that she was a fraud without actually saying it.

She gripped the tapestry chair arms, resisting the impulse to surge to her feet. "I'm not making any claims. I don't expect anything from Mr. Manning. I just want to know if it's true that his son was my father."

Twenty-nine years. That was how long Aunt Ella had known about her mother's marriage and kept it from her. Corrie could only marvel that she hadn't pressed for answers earlier. She'd simply accepted what Aunt Ella said—that her mother had come home to Ulee, Wyoming, pregnant, at eighteen. That she'd died in an accident when Corrie was six months old. That her mother had loved her.

Pain clutched her heart. Was that any more true than the rest of the fairy tale?

The attorneys exchanged glances. "You must realize," one of them began.

She shot to her feet. "Never mind what I must realize." Coming on top of the struggle to stretch her teaching salary and the meager income from Last Chance Café to pay Aunt Ella's hospital bills and funeral expenses, she didn't think she could handle any further runaround. "I'm done here. If Mr. Manning is interested in talking to me, he knows where to reach me. I'll be on my way."

She was halfway to the door when the voice stopped her.

"Come back here, young woman."

She turned, pulse accelerating. The man who'd come out of the suite's bedroom was older than either of the lawyers—in his seventies, at least. Slight and white-haired, his pallid skin declared his fragility, but he stood as straight as a man half his age.

"Mr. Manning." It had to be.

He lifted silvery eyebrows. "Aren't you going to call me 'Grandfather'?"

"No."

He let out a short laugh. "Fair enough, as I have no intention of letting you." He extended his hand to one of the attorneys without looking. The man gave him the copies she'd brought of her mother's marriage certificate and her own birth certificate.

"The birth certificate doesn't name a father." He zeroed in on the blank line, his gaze inimical.

She'd learned, over the years, to brace herself for that reaction whenever she had to produce a birth certificate. *You're a child of God,* Aunt Ella would say. *Let that be enough for you.*

Not exactly what a crying eight-year-old had wanted to hear, but typical of the tough Christian woman who'd raised her. Ella Grant had taken what life dished out without complaint, even when that meant bringing up an orphaned great-niece with little money and no help.

"According to my great-aunt, when I was born after my father died, my mother was afraid her husband's family would try to take me away. Later, she decided that they had a right to know." She kept her gaze steady on the man who might be her grandfather. "*You* had a right to know. She left for Savannah to talk to you about me when I was six months old. She died in an accident on the trip."

An accident—that was what Aunt Ella had always said. It was what Corrie had always believed, until she'd been sorting through Aunt Ella's papers after her stroke. She'd found the marriage license and a scribbled postcard, knocking down her belief in who she was like a child's tower of blocks.

He made a dismissive gesture with the papers. "Grace Grant never returned to Savannah after my son died." His voice grated on the words. With grief? She couldn't be sure. "If you are her daughter, that still doesn't guarantee my son was your father."

Her temper flared at the slur, but before she could speak, one of the lawyers did.

"A DNA test," he murmured.

Manning shot him an annoyed look. "From what I've learned, that's not likely to be conclusive with the intervening generation gone."

"Nevertheless—" The lawyer's smooth manner was slightly ruffled. Obviously the attorneys would prefer that he let them deal with this situation.

"I have no objection to a DNA test." Why would she, if there was even a chance that it would answer her questions?

Who am I, Lord? I know I'm Your child, but I have to know more.

Manning tossed the papers on the table, bracing himself with one hand on its glossy surface. "It doesn't matter. You won't get anything from me in any event."

"I don't want anything." That was what they seemed incapable of understanding. "All I want is to know something about my father. Nothing else."

His mouth twisted. "Do you really think I'll believe that?"

The truth sank in. Manning didn't believe her, and he wouldn't help her.

"No, obviously you can't." She wouldn't offer to shake hands. If her father had been anything like this man, maybe she was lucky he'd never been a part of her life. "I can't say it's been nice meeting you, Mr. Manning, but it's been interesting."

She turned toward the door again, holding her head high. Aunt Ella wouldn't have expected anything less. But the disappointment dragged like a weight pressing her down, compounding her still-raw grief.

"Just a minute." Manning's voice stopped her again. "I have a proposition for you."

"Proposition?" She turned back slowly, not sure she wanted to hear anything else he had to say.

A thin smile creased his lips. "I won't claim you as a grandchild, understand that. I won't give you anything. But you may come and stay at my house in Savannah for a few weeks." The lawyers were twittering, but he ignored them. "If you mean what you say, that will give you a chance to learn something about my son."

"If you don't believe I'm your grandchild, why would you want me there?" She eyed him, wondering what was in his mind.

His smile grew a bit unpleasant. "Ever heard the expression, 'putting a cat among the pigeons'? I suppose not. Never mind my motives. They are not your concern."

"Mr. Manning, we really don't think this is a good idea." Courtland and Broadbent exchanged glances.

Manning transferred his grip from the table to the back of the chair, leaning heavily, obviously tiring. "You make the arrangements. She can go now, while I'm still out of town. Lucas will take care of her."

"Lucas?" She grasped at the unfamiliar name, trying to make sense of this.

"Lucas Santee. He was married to my niece's child. He runs my companies."

"The young woman hasn't agreed to go." And the lawyers obviously hoped she wouldn't.

"She will." Manning sent her a shrewd glance. "Won't you?"

She didn't like his attitude. Didn't like the feeling that he was manipulating her for some reason she couldn't understand. If she acted on instinct, she'd walk right out the door and go back to Ulee. She had plenty there to keep her busy until school started again.

But she wouldn't, because if she did, she'd never know the answers to the questions that haunted her. *I hope this is what You want, Lord.*

"I'll go," she said.

Corrie leaned against the leather seat of the town car that had been waiting at the airport in Savannah. From the window, everything was so much softer, more verdant than she'd expected. Palmettos lined the road, and beyond them she could see rank after rank of tall, straight pines.

"Too bad the azaleas are past their prime." The grizzled driver, Jefferson, he'd said his name was, turned from the highway onto a residential street. "I always say you haven't seen Savannah until you've seen it with the azaleas blooming."

She watched the city flow by—streets lined with cream-colored walls, wrought-iron fences, twisted live oaks draped with silvery Spanish moss. Flowers bloomed everywhere, so lush and colorful they almost looked artificial. The houses seemed to hide behind their colorful barrier, as if holding secrets closed to her.

"Does the family live in this section of town?"

Jefferson nodded. "Not far. This here's the old part of

town." He waved a hand vaguely toward the left. "River Street's over that way. You'll want to see that while you're here. Right now I'm to stop and pick up Mr. Lucas, then take y'all to the house."

Corrie's nerves tingled. Manning had said Santee ran his company. What else did he run? Santee obviously intended to vet her before exposing the rest of the family to her. She felt a tingle of apprehension. "Are we picking him up at his office?"

"At the construction site. They've been having problems at the new building. Nothing Mr. Lucas can't handle. He can handle anything."

That was another view of Lucas Santee. He could handle anything. Maybe the implication was that he could handle her, too. In a moment she'd have a chance to decide for herself just how much of a challenge Lucas Santee was going to be.

Thanks to the briefing the lawyers had reluctantly provided, she knew that a number of Savannah businesses bore the Manning name. Lucas Santee ran the largest, the construction firm, and oversaw the rest since Manning's retirement.

The driver stopped the car next to a wooden construction barrier. "Here we are, miss. I'll just go find Mr. Lucas."

Jefferson disappeared into the construction site, but Corrie was too restless to wait. She was keyed up and ready. The plane trip had been a prelude. Her quest was about to start. She slid out of the car and followed Jefferson on to the construction site.

The three stories of what was going to be a new bank, according to the sign, were at the stark girder stage. The building loomed over her, surrounded by heavy yellow construction vehicles.

She didn't see Jefferson, so she smiled at the nearest worker. "Where's Lucas Santee?"

The man gave her the once-over before pointing to the third level of the building. "Up there. The suit."

Actually, Lucas Santee had shed his suit coat, but Corrie understood. The other man was short, round and rumpled in workmen's overalls. Santee's shirt was dazzling white, and his dark slacks had a knife-edge crease she could see from here. He stood confidently on a girder, as self-assured as if he stood in a boardroom.

Santee said something that looked emphatic, motioning to the building around him. The other man appeared to object, but Santee cut him off with a quick, definitive gesture.

Santee stepped into the open cage of an elevator. With one hand braced against the metal on either side, he descended. Was he looking her way? She couldn't be sure.

The cage jolted to a stop, and he stepped out lightly. He took a suit coat from the outstretched hand of one of his lackeys and handed over the yellow hard hat he'd been wearing.

Jefferson leaned close, murmuring something, and Santee sent a sharp glance at her before turning back to his men. He kept her waiting a few more minutes while he conferred with several people. Finally he detached himself from the group and started toward the car. He stepped from the shadow of the building, and the late-afternoon sun hit him like a spotlight.

Golden, that was the only word that came to mind. The sun tipped brown hair with gold. Even his tanned skin seemed to have a golden sheen. He covered the space between them in an unhurried, controlled stride.

Corrie's nerves tightened. He reminded her of a mountain lion. There was that same sense of feline grace, of muscles rippling under smooth, golden skin, of danger hidden under a shining surface.

Santee stopped a few feet from her, surveying her from top to toe. Looking for Manning family resemblance? Or just trying to intimidate her?

"Ms. Grant," he said finally, his voice a lazy baritone drawl. "I'm Lucas Santee."

He held out his hand, and after an infinitesimal pause, Corrie took it. His fingers were warm and callused against her skin, surprising her. Surely he didn't actually work with those hands.

"Guess I should say welcome to Savannah," he said. "Your ancestral home, if Baxter Manning isn't making the biggest mistake of his life in believing you."

Corrie stiffened at the flash of steel under the lazy drawl. She pulled her hand away. "If Mr. Manning wants to invite me here, I can't see that it's any of your concern."

Santee's eyebrows lifted. "Anything that affects the family concerns me. Especially a con artist trying to convince a sick old man she's his long-lost granddaughter."

Somehow it sounded even more insulting in his molasses-slow drawl, though she ought to be getting used to the doubt by now. "I've told the lawyers and Mr. Manning. Now I'll tell you. I don't want anything from him."

"No secret dreams of being the missing heiress, coming into all that lovely money?"

"Obviously the money is important to you. Not to me. I agreed to this visit to find out about my father. Nothing more."

He smiled slowly, his eyes intent on her face, as if he tried to see beneath the surface. "Then we have to make sure you enjoy your time here, don't we?" He took her arm, the warmth of his grip penetrating her sleeve. "Jefferson's waiting," he said. "Shall we go?"

Corrie had expected a bigger battle, and this swift surrender took her off guard, leaving her with nothing to say. She slanted a look at Lucas Santee's face as he walked beside her to the car.

No, not surrender. Round One might have ended, but behind that smooth facade Lucas Santee was gearing up for future battles. This had just been a minor skirmish.

He held the door and then slid onto the leather seat next to her. The car purred onto the street.

Corrie stared out the window, acutely aware of the man beside her. Obviously she hadn't thought this through enough. She hadn't anticipated the hostility of people who feared she was trying to take what was theirs.

She straightened, pressing her back into the cool leather. These people had had it easy all their lives. Maybe that was behind Baxter Manning's odd attitude—he wanted to expose them to the uncertainty most people lived with.

She glanced at Santee and found him watching her. His eyes were an odd shade of brown up close, with flecks of gold that made them look like amber.

"Plotting your strategy?" His voice was pitched for her ears only, even though Jefferson had closed the glass partition. "Thinking about how you're going to worm your way into the heart of the family, so to speak?"

She felt anger color her cheeks. "I'm not trying to convince anybody of anything."

"Right. You're willing to travel across the country to move in with people who'll hate you on sight, but you're not trying to convince anybody you're Baxter Manning's grandchild." His fingers closed around her wrist. "Try that story on someone who might believe it, sugar."

Corrie stiffened. His intensity grated on her, but she wouldn't let him think he intimidated her.

"Your opinion doesn't really matter, does it?" she said. "The only thing that matters is what Mr. Manning believes."

His grip tightened until she thought he'd leave fingerprints on her skin, and fury darkened his eyes. "Baxter Manning wants to think he's found an unknown grandchild, but you and I know differently, don't we?"

"Do we?" Corrie raised her eyebrows. At least she'd managed to dent that facade of his.

"I don't know who you really are, Corrie Grant. But I'll find out, I promise you that."

It didn't sound like a promise. It sounded like a threat.

He'd let this woman ruffle him, Lucas realized, and that shouldn't have happened. Dealing with her was going to be a delicate matter, particularly since he hadn't been able to tell what Baxter really thought of her from their brief phone conversation.

That was typical of Baxter, of course. He'd run his companies and his family with an iron hand all his life, and he didn't intend to let advancing age or illness stop him. He'd been maddeningly vague when Lucas tried to find out what he really thought of Corrie Grant.

Take care of her, he'd said. *Let her see what she can find out about Trey. That's what she says she wants to do.*

Trey Manning. He had a few vague memories of Trey, the golden boy who'd been a prep school athlete when Lucas had come to the Manning house as a child. Trey had been the only person who'd ever successfully stood up to Baxter, and look how that had ended.

And now this woman had come, claiming to be Trey's daughter. Worry gnawed at him. Baxter was too old and, he suspected, too ill to be on guard. So he had to protect the family.

The thought sent a wave of weariness over him. That had become a full-time job since Julia's death, and he didn't expect it would ever end.

The car drew smoothly to the curb and stopped. He roused himself and opened the door, holding it for Corrie. "Welcome to Savannah," he said again, knowing she understood how little he welcomed her.

Corrie slid onto the sidewalk and just stood for a moment, looking at the graceful sweep of steps with their glossy black wrought-iron railing. Visualizing herself owning the place, perhaps? Or feeling reluctant to go in and face what waited for her there?

"This is Mr. Manning's house?"

"It is." He almost imagined that was a bit of awe in her clear blue eyes, but that hardly seemed likely. An accomplished fraud would surely have boned up on the place.

Maybe it was those big blue eyes that had caught Baxter's attention. Trey had had the blue eyes and curling blond hair, too. But not the freckles that dusted Corrie's lightly tanned cheeks or the snub nose that made her look like a classic girl next door, if the girl next door happened to be a con artist.

"I didn't realize…" She stopped, as if unwilling to share whatever she didn't realize with him.

"That it was so old?"

She slanted a sideways glance at him, nodding.

"The house was built in 1835 in classic Regency style

and restored in the early sixties when the historic district was in the midst of a wave of preservation." He launched into the familiar recital. If you lived in Savannah's historic district, you could do it in your sleep. "The compound has four town houses, built around a shared courtyard. Baxter lives here, and Eulalie Ashworth, his niece, has the next one." He nodded to the adjoining house, identical in design and decor.

"I see." She looked as if she were trying to take it all in. Maybe she never had been out of Wyoming. If so, Savannah was going to be a shock.

"The two houses that face the alley are smaller but similar in design. My son and I live in one. The other one is rented to a family friend, Lydia Baron." He paused for an instant. "That was originally Trey's house."

He thought there was a small intake of breath, but otherwise she didn't react. Maybe she was tougher than she looked.

"Shall we go in?" He gestured to the curving stairway.

Corrie hesitated. Then, with her face wooden, she started up.

He followed, running his hand along the polished rail. He couldn't help but love introducing his city to a stranger, even an unwelcome one like Corrie. Savannah was bred in him. For all the city's faults, he'd be a foreigner anywhere else.

"The main floor in many of Savannah's historic homes is on the second floor—the parlor floor. The downstairs is called the garden level."

She paused in front of the glossy black door. Heavy pots of alyssum stood on either side of it, perfuming the air. "I understand Mr. Manning hasn't returned yet."

Corrie, naturally, would be more concerned with the man she hoped to impress than with the decor.

"Not yet." He reached past her to turn the brass knob. "But I'm sure some of the family is waiting to meet you."

And ready to behave, he hoped. He'd warned all of them not to give this woman any ammunition to use against them with Baxter. He could just hope they'd paid attention.

He opened the door. They stepped into the long entrance hallway, rich with the mingled aromas of polish and potpourri. Two people waited for them: Eulalie, his mother-in-law; Deidre Ashworth, his sister-in-law. He shot Deidre a warning look.

"Eulalie, this is Corrie Grant." He smiled reassuringly at Eulalie, knowing she was torn between her innate Southern courtesy and her fear that Corrie would somehow supplant her two children. "Corrie, this is Eulalie Ashworth, Mr. Manning's niece. Who may, or may not, be your...let's see, second cousin."

"Of course she is not our cousin." Deidre took a step forward, hands curling into fists as if she'd like to throw Corrie out bodily. "She's a fraud, and she's not welcome in this house."

TWO

Corrie froze for an instant. Obviously she should have been ready for direct hostility, but she wasn't. What had happened to that Southern hospitality she'd heard so much about?

She stiffened her spine. Aunt Ella had taught her how to behave, and she wouldn't shame her. She held out her hand to the older of the two women, trying to manage a smile.

Eulalie Ashworth was as soft and round and fluffy as a mound of cotton candy. She also looked perplexed. She studied Corrie's hand as if it might be a deadly weapon and then took it. Corrie felt soft, powdery skin and smelled a whiff of lilac scent.

"Welcome to Savannah..." Eulalie began, but the younger woman interrupted.

"She's not welcome. I don't see any reason why we should be polite."

"An accusation no one could possibly make about you, Deidre." Lucas smiled, but Corrie thought his amber eyes held a warning. "Corrie, this is Eulalie's daughter, Deidre Ashworth."

Deidre obviously wouldn't take her hand. Her eyes flashed with anger, and her dark hair fairly sparked with electricity. Midtwenties, at a guess, she was sharp, thin, brittle and beautifully dressed.

"Deidre. Mr. Manning mentioned you."

Deidre lifted arched black brows. "Not calling him Grandfather already? How subtle of you."

"I've already told Lucas. Now I'll tell you." She darted a glance at Lucas. He leaned broad shoulders against the newel post of the soaring staircase, watching her with a sardonic expression. "I don't want anything except to find out about my parents."

"As I said, how subtle." Deidre was clearly not impressed. She swung on Lucas, as if he were to blame. "Do we really have to have this creature in our house?"

"Deidre, please." Eulalie's cheeks turned as pink as her dress. "Think what Uncle Baxter would say."

Deidre glared at her mother. "Uncle Baxter must have entered his second childhood. We should have him declared incompetent."

Corrie's head began to throb. Maybe Baxter Manning had overestimated his control over his family. If they didn't cooperate, she'd find out nothing.

"This is Baxter's home." Lucas's voice hadn't lost its lazy timbre, but there was steel underneath. "It's up to him to say who stays here. And need I remind you who owns the house you live in?"

For a moment the fury in Deidre's face was so out of control Corrie thought she'd strike him. Her hands clenched until the veins stood out. "You'd take Uncle Baxter's side, of course. You always do. But then, you know which side your bread is buttered on, don't you, Lucas?"

If the barb hurt, Lucas didn't show it. "It's common sense, Deidre, which you seem to be sadly lacking."

The side door into the hall swung open.

"Grandma, is she here yet?" A small figure ran into the hallway. The boy threw himself at Lucas. "Is she, Daddy?"

Lucas caught the child, lifting him high in the air. For an instant Lucas's face was open, and the love when he looked at his son touched a surprising chord in Corrie.

Was that what she really wanted from this trip? Some sign that the father she'd never known would have loved her?

"Please, Lucas. Put Jason down." Eulalie fluttered toward them, hands outstretched as if to take a baby. "That's not good for him."

Not good for him? The words startled Corrie. Was something wrong with the boy? He looked like a normal six-year-old, fair and a little skinny, as active kids often were at that age.

But Lucas set him down immediately, something that might have been guilt flickering in his face. He brushed the boy's silky blond hair back from his forehead gently.

"He's all right. Corrie, this is my son, Jason. He's eight."

Corrie mentally adjusted her image of the child. He was a bit small for eight. He came forward to shake hands solemnly.

"Hi, Jason." At last, someone who didn't seem to be out to get her. She smiled at him.

"Hello, Cousin Corrie."

Deidre jerked as if she'd been shot. "Don't call her cousin, Jason. She's not your cousin."

"But Grandma said that Uncle Baxter said—"

"Just call me Corrie, okay?" She wouldn't let a child be pulled into their quarrel. "I'm glad to meet you, Jason."

His mother had been Deidre's older sister—she knew

that from the briefing the attorneys had given her. Julia, her name was. She'd died three years earlier.

Jason studied her, brown eyes grave. "You don't look like a cowgirl." He sounded disappointed.

Eulalie drew in a scandalized breath, but Corrie just smiled. Cowgirl was probably the least of the things the family had been calling her.

"Well, even cowgirls get a little dressed up to travel. My boots are in my luggage."

Jason's small face lit with a smile. "Maybe we can go riding while you're here. My daddy's a good rider. He's won lots of ribbons."

That was an unexpected sidelight on Lucas. "He's probably better than I am, then."

"Jason, you know you're not allowed to ride," Eulalie said. She frowned at Corrie, as if this were her fault.

"If we might get the conversation off horses, maybe we could decide what we're doing." Deidre poked furiously at the silver bowl of lilacs on the drop-leaf table.

"There's no decision to be made. We're going to do exactly what Baxter asked." Lucas's gaze rested on Corrie with a challenge. "I'm sure things will work out just as they should."

In other words, he intended to expose her for a fraud.

She met his look defiantly. "Things usually do."

His eyes darkened. For a moment the air between them sizzled with antagonism and some other emotion Corrie didn't care to name. It was as if there was no one else in the room.

Lucas took a deliberate step back. Once again, Corrie had managed to get under his guard. He didn't like it. He wouldn't allow it.

Eulalie fluttered toward the archway, breaking the spell. "I don't know why we're all standing here in the hall. Come into the parlor, and we'll have tea. I'm sure Corrie needs refreshment after her long trip."

Deidre looked as if she'd like to slam out of the house. At his warning frown, she glared back, but then she turned and followed Eulalie.

He'd known from the moment Baxter told them about Corrie that Deidre would cause trouble. He sometimes had trouble remembering the lively little girl she'd been when he'd first started seeing her sister. Deidre had grown into a perennially dissatisfied young woman, and he didn't know why.

He followed the women into the front parlor, holding Jason's hand, and watched Corrie to see what she'd make of the place. She paused as she reached the edge of the Kirman carpet and looked the length of the room—actually adjoining parlors, divided by white Ionic columns that supported the central arch. The period furniture Baxter had collected over a lifetime was a fitting complement to the matching marble fireplaces.

"Beautiful."

He was probably the only one who heard the breathed comment. "Home, sweet home," he murmured.

He saw the color come up under her tan, but she didn't look at him. She crossed instead to the brocade love seat and sat, head held high.

Eulalie poured Earl Grey from the Revere teapot. Obviously she'd decided to treat Corrie as an honored guest, since she'd had Baxter's housekeeper get out the fragile china cups that had come to Savannah on an eighteenth-century merchant ship. Either that, or she was attempting to make Corrie feel like a fish out of water.

It was hard to tell. Eulalie had her Savannah lady face on, and no one did it better. She passed a cup and saucer to Corrie. "I hope you had a pleasant flight."

Corrie balanced the fragile cup and saucer, looking as if tea-party conversation was beyond her. She took a breath and seemed to rally. "Not bad. Long."

Deidre put two spoons of sugar in her cup, ignoring her mother's frown. Eulalie didn't need to worry. Deidre wore off everything she ate with that endless fidgeting of hers. Julia had been exactly the opposite—calm, serene, never troubling herself about anything that didn't directly concern her.

"Where does one fly from to get out of Wyoming?" Deidre's voice was edged with sarcasm.

He'd have to have another talk with her. There was a line between wanting to expose Corrie as a fraud and giving her an excuse to complain to Baxter about them.

"Actually, I flew out of Rapid City, South Dakota. That's the closest airport to Ulee." Corrie seemed to have her temper well in hand.

"I'm afraid I've never heard of Ulee, Wyoming." Deidre made it sound like the back of beyond, which he supposed it was. Still, plenty of people thought of Savannah as a quaint backwater, notable only for its antebellum charm.

Corrie put her cup down with an audible click. "That's where my mother and father met and married," she said. "I should have thought that would occasion plenty of comment."

Of course it had. He hadn't been old enough to care at the time, but he'd heard plenty about it later. Trey, taking a summer off to tour the country, had met a waitress in the wilds of Wyoming and married her in less than a month, then foolishly expected his father to welcome her. He should have known better.

He was mildly amused at the expression on Deidre's face, but maybe it was time to intervene. He didn't care to be treated to another example of Deidre's temper.

"Has anyone seen Ainsley? I expected him to be here."

"I—I am here, Lucas."

Ainsley paused in the archway, looking as if he'd like any excuse to turn and go away again. Lucas couldn't blame him for wanting to avoid the fireworks Deidre enjoyed, but he did wish Ainsley would sometimes act like a responsible grown-up instead of a shy kid.

"We missed you at work today." He tried to keep his voice even, but some of the exasperation he felt probably came through. Pushing Ainsley into a job as Lucas's assistant when he was just out of college wasn't the smartest move Baxter had ever made. The boy wasn't cut out for the business world.

Ainsley's gaze evaded his. "I told your secretary I wasn't well."

"You seem to have recovered."

"I thought I'd go for a walk, okay?" Ainsley flared up, sounding like a sulky teenager. "I always do that when I'm getting over a migraine."

"Of course you do, dear." Eulalie patted the love seat. "Sit here and let me pour you some tea. Everyone knows how you suffer from migraines."

The look Eulalie shot at Lucas dared him to disagree. He wanted to. *You've spoiled Ainsley with your constant coddling, and now you're doing the same with my son.*

But he couldn't say that. He'd been wrong about Julia, and the guilt would hang around his neck for the rest of his life. He wouldn't risk being wrong about Jason.

"This is Corrie," Eulalie went on. "I knew you'd be back to meet her."

Ainsley nodded, polite but disinterested. He'd seemed detached from the fierce family discussions that had raged since Baxter broke the news.

Lucas glanced at Corrie, to find she was leaning toward his son, listening to something Jason was saying, undoubtedly about horses. The tenderness on her face jolted him.

Corrie didn't have any right looking at his son that way. And Baxter didn't have any right foisting this stranger off on the family. The least he could do was come back and deal with her himself.

"Jason." The desire to get his son away from Corrie was probably irrational, but he couldn't help himself. "It's time we were getting home, son."

The animation faded from Jason's face as he slid off the seat. "Goodbye, Cousin Corrie. I'll see you later."

Deidre's lips tightened, but he silenced her with a glance. He didn't require Deidre's input. He could take care of his son himself.

The way you took care of Julia? The small voice in his mind inquired.

He turned to thank Eulalie, but she had become involved in arbitrating a heated exchange between Ainsley and Deidre, much as she'd done when they were small. Corrie's eyes met his, and he realized from the amusement in them that she was thinking much the same thing.

That jolted him. She shouldn't look at him as if they understood each other.

"Thank you for introducing me to…" There was the faintest hesitation in her voice, as if she balked at thinking of them as her family. "…to Mr. Manning's family," she went on smoothly. "I'm sure I'll be seeing you again."

He leaned toward her. "Of course you will. I wouldn't think of missing dinner on your first night here. At Eulalie's house, at eight. We've invited someone who knew Trey well."

And who won't like your pretence any more than we do.

Corrie's polite smile seemed to stiffen. "I'll look forward to it."

He could imagine. "Not so easy, is it?" He lowered his voice, not that the others would notice. They were well away with their own quarrel by now. "Always on your guard, pretending to be someone you're not."

"I don't have to pretend." Her chin lifted, and her eyes challenged him.

"I guess we'll see about that, won't we?"

Before she could answer, Ainsley's tenor voice soared out of the babble.

"Stop trying to make me over. I'm not Trey, and Uncle Baxter is never going to treat me as if I am."

The silence that followed was deafening. Lucas felt the despairing frustration that his wife's family so often brought to the fore. It was as if he were the only adult in a roomful of children. Why didn't they just hand Baxter's inheritance to the woman on a silver platter?

Eulalie's eyes were bright with tears. "I'm sure I don't know what you're talking about, Ainsley. All I want is for you to be happy."

For a moment he thought Ainsley would flare out at his mother, but he retreated into sulky silence instead. Surprisingly, it was Corrie who returned them to a semblance of normalcy.

"I'd really like to freshen up from the trip, so if you wouldn't mind…"

Recalled to her hostess duties, Eulalie hustled to her feet. "I'll show you to your room."

He stepped back to let Corrie pass him. "I'll see you at dinner, then."

And maybe by then he'd have at least a preliminary report from the private investigator who was supposed to be finding out everything there was to know about Corrie Grant.

"That's the lot of them." Corrie leaned back on the four-poster bed, cell phone cradled against her ear. She'd just finished giving Ann Moreno a rundown of her reception. If she hadn't been able to confide in her closest friend, she'd have burst. "And every one of them would like nothing better than to run me out of town."

"You didn't go to Savannah to make them like you," Ann said. "What matters is finding out about your parents."

She could always count on Ann for a sensible approach, and she felt a wave of longing to be sitting across from her at a scrubbed table in the café, chatting over the coffee cups.

"I just hope someone's willing to talk about them. So far I haven't seen any signs of that."

"It's early days yet. You'll work it out. Meanwhile, don't worry about anything here."

"Thanks, Annie. I couldn't do this if you hadn't taken over the café."

"You'd do the same for me, if I ever discovered I was a lost heiress." Ann's chuckle was warm. "Not that it's very likely. You take care, honey."

Corrie hung up, comforted. Someone, at least, had

confidence in her. She glanced at her watch. Time to get dressed for dinner at Eulalie's.

If someone back home said come on over to supper, she knew what that meant. Here, she wasn't sure. She began to dress, hoping a denim skirt would do.

A nap and a shower had helped. She no longer felt so tense. She could even enjoy the bedroom, with its four-poster bed and cool white walls. The floral print of the bed skirt was echoed in the drapes on the many-paned windows that looked out onto the courtyard, seeming to invite the greenery in.

Taking her well-worn Bible from the suitcase, she put it on the mahogany bedside table and opened it to Psalms. The single, faded photograph of her parents she'd found among Aunt Ella's papers looked back at her.

She picked it up, studying the young faces. Gracie smiled at her brand-new husband, her eyes soft with love. Laughter lit Trey's lean face as he looked at his bride. They'd been newlyweds, ready to leave for Savannah so that Gracie could meet his family. What had happened in a few short months here to bring them to such a tragic end?

She had to know. She tucked the photograph back inside the Bible and closed it. She would know.

Closing the bedroom door behind her, she paused at the top of the graceful curving staircase. Sunlight streamed through French doors that opened onto a balcony from the spacious upper hallway, and pink roses in a silver urn perfumed the air.

Father, I know You've brought me here for a reason. Please, lead me to the people who have answers.

She went down the curving stairway, running her hand along the polished railing. Her soft footsteps on the carpet made little sound, and the crystal chandelier in the down-stairs hall tinkled once in response and then was still.

"I hope being alone in the house won't bother you," Eulalie had said. "Mrs. Andrews does sleep in, but I'm afraid she's so deaf she wouldn't hear anything softer than the last trumpet."

Corrie had already met the housekeeper, who'd regarded her with the deepest suspicion and pretended to be unable to hear anything Corrie said. If Lucas and company thought the possibility of being virtually alone was enough to scare her away, they'd better think again.

The long downstairs hallway bisected the house, leading onto a glassed-in porch that overlooked the garden. She went through it and down the curved, wrought-iron stairs. A small brick patio was flanked by flower beds overflow-ing with peonies and old-fashioned roses, and the railing supported such a lush growth of ivy that it threatened to take over the stairs.

The wall of Eulalie's house formed the backdrop of the flower beds. Lovely, she supposed, but the place made her feel claustrophobic. Why did they want to live in such close quarters? Even the air was close, heavy with mois-ture. She could feel her hair curling in reaction.

She followed the brick pathway toward Eulalie's door. A fountain splashed softly in the middle of the garden, and beyond it, half-hidden by the foliage, were the other two houses, a little smaller, less grand than the two that faced the street.

One of them had been the house where her parents lived during their brief time here together. It was rented to an old family friend, according to Lucas. If she could see it...

But what would that tell her after thirty years? It couldn't tell her if they'd been happy there, or if Trey had known about Gracie's pregnancy. Would he have been glad?

The door swung open, as if someone had been watching. The sight of Lucas cut short a line of fruitless speculation.

"Corrie, come in. We've been waiting for you."

That should have sounded welcoming. It didn't.

An interminable hour and a half later they'd moved from Eulalie's formal dining room to an equally formal front parlor. Like Baxter's parlor next door, this one was furnished with antiques, but the effect in Eulalie's room was crowded, rather than spacious, as if she hadn't been able to resist the attraction of just one more crystal vase or china figurine.

The dinner guest Lucas had mentioned now patted a spot next to her on a plush love seat. "Come and sit next to me, Corrie. We must chat."

There was nothing Corrie would like better, because Lydia Baron was the family friend who rented Trey's house. Trey and Gracie's house, she mentally corrected. Surely her mother had had the right to think of it as hers when she'd lived there.

She sat down, aware of the comparison between her denim and the silk dress the other woman wore. Lydia must be about Eulalie's age, but in contrast to Eulalie's soft, faded charm, Lydia had a brisk, down-to-earth manner and a slim, athletic frame that a younger woman might have envied. Her gray hair was short and stylish, and bright blue eyes sparkled in a tanned face.

"What are you thinking of all of us, I wonder?" Lydia sounded amused. "Pitchforked into the midst of Baxter's dysfunctional family as you are."

"Dysfunctional?" She'd pegged Lydia as forthright, but this seemed a little too blunt, even for a family friend.

"What can I say?" Lydia lowered her voice, but Corrie doubted anyone heard them over the wrangle Deidre and Ainsley had just begun. "You can see for yourself. No one's happy."

Corrie looked over that comment for hidden traps. She'd like to believe she'd found someone who'd be honest with her, but it hardly seemed possible that Lydia would take her side against the family.

"Brothers and sisters often argue, I guess. I don't have any siblings, so I can't say for sure."

"Ainsley and Deidre fight with each other because they don't want to hurt their mother's soft heart. They're afraid to take their quarrel to the real source of their unhappiness. Baxter Manning."

Here was blunt speaking with a vengeance. "I'm not sure I understand what you mean," she said cautiously.

"Baxter has to rule the roost, surely you've figured that out about him. Ainsley must have a job with the company, because that's what Baxter expects, even though the boy would rather dabble with his drawings." She dismissed Ainsley with a glance. "Meanwhile Deidre, who actually might accomplish something in the business, is left clerking in a genteel shop, waiting to make the proper marriage."

Corrie blinked. "Do you mean they listen to him? That sounds like something out of the last century."

"Baxter is something out of the last century. And since he controls the purse strings, everyone has to do what he wishes or risk losing his support. There are periodic rebellions, but so far no one has actually broken away."

Corrie's gaze sought out Lucas. He'd propped his tall figure against a cherry armoire and frowned across the room at her.

"That doesn't include Lucas."

"Even Lucas." Lydia's eyes were bright with what might have been either interest or malice. "In theory Lucas runs Baxter's companies, but in actual practice he can't make a single decision without being second-guessed."

Lucas didn't impress her as a man who'd allow himself to be dictated to, but she didn't really know him, did she? And if he had his way, she never would.

"And then there's you." Lydia's smile held an edge.

"What about me?"

"Didn't you realize, my dear? Baxter doesn't care a snap if you're his long-lost granddaughter or not. He's sent you here as a threat, to show the others what might happen to all that lovely money if they don't do what he says."

THREE

Corrie took a deep breath as she reached the bottom of the stairs, leaving Eulalie's dinner party behind. All she wanted now was out, away from all those people with their inimical faces and their crosscurrents of emotion. Then the steps behind her creaked, and she realized that Lucas had followed her down.

"Haven't you baited me enough for one night?" She was too annoyed to try to be polite.

He lifted his hands in surrender. "I'm just on my way home myself. Did you like getting the lowdown on all of us from Lydia?"

She still hadn't decided what she thought about the woman's comments and wouldn't tell Lucas in any event. "Lydia was kind enough to ask me to drop in on her. She realized I might want to see where my mother lived when she was here."

"Did she now? I wonder what's going on in that shrewd brain of hers."

She glanced at his face in the low light from the fixture at the bottom of the stairs, but it didn't give anything away. Beyond him, the family room was dark with shadows. "Is she shrewd?"

"Definitely." He leaned against the door frame, apparently ready to talk. "She runs half the cultural boards in Savannah practically single-handed, and she took the demise of the symphony like a death in the family."

"You said she was an old family friend. Is that why Mr. Manning was willing to rent Trey's house to her? I'd think he probably wouldn't want a stranger living in such close quarters."

Lucas shrugged, glancing through the glass pane in the door toward the dark garden. Lights shone along the walks that divided the houses. "I suppose. Are you picturing it as yours?"

Exasperation swept through her like a wind off the mountains. "I'm telling you for approximately the hundredth time, I don't want anything. I'm just trying to understand why you all live so close together."

"I don't know why Lydia decided to rent the house. The families were always close, so maybe she felt at home here. Eulalie lives here because Baxter took her in when she married someone with more charm than money. We all preserve the fiction that she keeps house for him."

Lucas was being surprisingly open. Because his family had annoyed him with their constant bickering? Or was this yet another trap he was setting for her?

"And why do you live here?"

He frowned absently. "Baxter offered us the house when Julia and I married. She wanted to be close to her mother, and I was working twelve-hour days at the business. It seemed like a good idea. Why do you care? Are you storing up tales to spill to Baxter?"

"No. Why are you telling me? Are you trying to trip me up?"

He gave a reluctant laugh. "You're something, Corrie Grant. If that's who you really are."

"That's what my birth certificate says."

He was very close, the garden level very quiet. The faint sound of voices drifted down from the floor above. "Birth certificates can be faked."

"And fakes can be found out. Mine isn't. Why can't you see…"

She looked up and met his eyes. Whatever else she'd intended to say seemed to get lost, and her breath caught.

Lucas—she didn't even like him. So why should her heart be pounding and her breath ragged just because he stood so close, looked so intently?

He felt it, too. She could see it in the sudden darkening of his eyes.

She shook off the sensation. She was tired. Jet-lagged. She hadn't felt a thing. "I am exactly who I say I am," she said shortly. "Go ahead, investigate. You won't find anything else."

"Maybe not." If he'd felt anything, it was gone now. "You can be sure I'll try." He went quickly out into the garden, the door banging behind him.

She waited a moment or two, giving him time to get clear of the path. Then she stepped outside and took a deep breath of scented garden air. It was still muggy, but it felt good after the welter of emotions she'd been through today.

A wrought-iron bench curved beneath a magnolia tree as if it had grown there. She sank down on it, not ready to go in yet.

That sudden little spark of attraction had been a shock— one that neither of them expected or welcomed. Well, it was gone now, drifting away as if it had never been.

She sat for a while, barely thinking, just letting the peace of the garden seep into her. She'd questioned why they all lived here, but this garden in itself was a reason.

Finally, realizing how late it must be getting, she made her way slowly toward Baxter's house. Her feet made little sound on the brick path, and a dense growth of shrubbery enclosed her. Maybe that was why, when the voice came, it startled her so much.

"…she's my problem, not yours."

It took a moment to realize the voice belonged to Ainsley, another moment to understand that he was talking on a cell phone. He didn't sound stammering or diffident now.

"I know that." His voice was sharp. "Just stay out of it. This is my problem, and I'll take care of it."

He might mean anything, she assured herself, but his "she's my problem," seemed to ring in her ears. She was probably the only problem facing Ainsley right now, and the threat he thought she represented to his inheritance.

She felt chilled in spite of the warm, humid air. It was disturbing to be the target of so much ill will. Softly, not wanting another confrontation tonight, she slipped down the path and through the garden door.

Baxter's house closed silently around her. She'd thought the garden was quiet, but in comparison to the house, it had been alive with rustles and chirpings and murmurings. The house was silent, dead silent, and she was uneasily aware that, for all intents and purposes, she was alone here.

She'd been alone in scarier places than this—backpacking in the mountains, or keeping a midnight vigil beside Aunt Ella's bed those last few nights. She wouldn't give in to fear.

The darkness and the light are both alike to Thee. The

words of the Psalm came to her mind without conscious thought, and she started up the stairs.

The parlor floor lay black and empty, save for a small lamp Mrs. Andrews had left on in the hallway. Moonlight from the landing window traced a path down the stairwell. She paused, hand on the railing. That sound—was it a footfall from somewhere on the bedroom floor?

"Mrs. Andrews?" Her voice was tentative, although there was no one to disturb with her call.

Nothing. The house was as still as an old house ever is.

She went quickly up the steps before she could imagine anything else. No one was here. No one could be here.

Still, it felt good to close the bedroom door behind her and switch on the light. The cozy room sprang to life in its soft glow.

They'd laugh if they thought they'd managed to spook her, and she wouldn't give them the satisfaction.

She crossed to the dresser, taking off her watch, and then paused in the act of laying it down. She pulled open one drawer, and then another.

There was no mistaking the signs. Her room had been searched. The searcher had been careful, but not careful enough. He'd left traces visible to someone as organized as she was.

Heart thumping, she went quickly through her belongings. Nothing seemed to be missing, but…

She hurried to the bedside table and opened the Bible. Her breath came out in a sigh of relief when she found the photo still there, the faces still smiling up at her.

She closed the Bible again, holding it against her chest for a moment. Everything had been searched—everything had been put back in its proper place.

Except for one thing. The notes she'd made about the family, based on the attorney's briefing—those were gone.

By the time she'd finished breakfast the next morning, Corrie had decided on her course of action. There was nothing useful she could do. Accusing anyone would only lead to a fruitless quarrel.

She walked out into the garden, relieved that the air seemed to have cleared a bit. A faint breeze rustled the palmettos and sent a shower of withered magnolia blossoms down on her.

Who had it been? Lucas? He could have seen her linger in the garden and taken the opportunity, although he couldn't have known how quickly she might have gone into the house. Deidre or Ainsley? They'd both come to dinner well after she'd arrived. That would have given them time. Even Eulalie could have done it, although she had trouble imagining Eulalie rushing out the front door as she went out the back.

It didn't really matter. The notes that had been taken proved nothing, except that she had been briefed before she arrived in Savannah. She couldn't even imagine what that unknown someone expected to prove by taking them.

She rounded a bend in the path and found herself face to-face with Ainsley. He looked up, startled, hand arrested on a sketch pad.

"C-Corrie. Good morning." The shy stammer was charming, as was the faint flush that rose under his tan at the sight of her. But she hadn't forgotten his incisive voice on the phone.

"Good morning." She moved a little closer, hoping for a glance at the sketch. "What are you drawing?"

"Nothing." He slapped the pad closed and planted his hands on top of it.

"Someone mentioned that you're very artistic. I'd love to see your work sometime."

"It's nothing but a hobby." His tone was just short of rude, and he shot off the bench where he'd been sitting. "I have to get to work."

He darted off as if she'd been chasing him, disappearing into the shrubbery. She didn't have a chance to point out that since today was Saturday, it was unlikely he had to go to work.

"Corrie." She turned at the sound of her name, to find Lydia standing near the fountain, waving. "I didn't expect to find you out this early. Would you care to come and see my house?"

Her house. Well, Lydia had a right to think of it that way. It hadn't been Gracie and Trey's house in a long time.

"Thanks." She crossed the garden quickly. "I'd like to."

There were faint shadows under Lydia's eyes, as if she hadn't had a restful night, and the lines in her face were more pronounced in the sunlight, but she still moved as lightly as a girl.

"Come in. I was taking my morning look at the garden."

"I can see why you'd want to. It's beautiful." Corrie followed her through the garden-level door. Inside, the space that was a sort of family room in Baxter's house was an efficient-looking office here.

"My work area." Lydia waved dismissively at a computer station and filing cabinets. "I'm on far too many boards and committees not to stay organized."

Corrie stopped at a cabinet filled with trophies—sailing, riding, shooting, tennis—apparently whatever Lydia did, she did well. "You're obviously quite a sportswoman."

"Don't believe that image of Southern women as belles who languish on the veranda, drinking mint juleps."

"I'm learning not to, but I have to confess, until I came here, I didn't know anything about Savannah except the clichés."

"You'll learn. Although I don't suppose you'll be here that long." She was already heading up the stairs, so apparently the comment didn't require an answer.

Corrie followed, wondering where Lydia stood in all this. She could be a disinterested party. Lucas had called her a family friend, but which member of the family had her loyalty?

"Did you know Trey very well?" she asked as they came out into the center hallway—smaller than the one in Baxter's house, but beautifully proportioned.

"My dear, Trey and I were close from the diaper stage on." Lydia smiled, but her mind seemed focused elsewhere. "Our mothers were best friends. Supposedly Trey kissed me in the sandbox at age two, and I boxed his ears."

"You must have been surprised when he married so suddenly."

Lydia considered, her head tilted to one side. "Not surprised that he rebelled against his father, no. Just a bit surprised that his rebellion took that form."

Corrie blinked. "My aunt said—" She stopped, not sure she wanted to repeat what Aunt Ella had said—that Trey had taken one look at Gracie and fallen head over heels in love.

"There he is." Lydia nodded to the wall above the staircase, and Corrie realized she meant the portrait that hung there. "Trey Manning, painted on his eighteenth birthday."

This wasn't the laughing, jeans-clad figure of her faded

photograph. This was a golden boy, someone who had the world in the palm of his hand and the confidence that went with it. He stood erect, hand placed carelessly on the back of a chair, staring at the artist with something she could only call arrogance. She thought she preferred the photo.

She had to say something. "I'm surprised it's here, rather than in Baxter's house."

Lydia was turned toward the portrait, so Corrie couldn't see her face. "It very nearly wasn't anywhere. Baxter told Mrs. Andrews to burn it."

"Burn it!" How could any father want to burn his son's portrait? "Why?"

"Anger. Sheer, unadulterated anger at Trey for disappointing him. Luckily Mrs. Andrews had sense enough to tell Eulalie, who came to me. I rescued it. I thought someday he'd want it back, but he never has."

She didn't need to ask what the disappointment was. Obviously Baxter hadn't wanted his son to marry an insignificant waitress when all of Savannah society was his for the taking.

She could add up two and two as well as the next person. Lydia had been right. Baxter had sent her here to push his family into doing his bidding with the threat of a new potential heir. Even if he became convinced she was Trey's child, he'd never welcome her.

Lydia swung back to face her. "I hope that doesn't put a bad taste in your mouth. Baxter's all right—one just has to know how to handle him. That was something Trey never mastered. He needed a wife who could do it for him."

"Meaning my mother couldn't?"

"I'm afraid she was too unhappy during her marriage to handle anyone."

"Unhappy? My aunt said that she and Trey were deliriously happy."

"Did she?" Lydia's voice was gentle. "Well, perhaps that's what she wanted to believe. I saw them both from the time they came back to this house. Oh, Trey put on a good front. He'd defied his father at last and gotten away with it, I suppose he thought. Grace knew better. She knew their marriage was destined to fail from the moment they got here."

The rest of Lydia's tour went over Corrie's head as she struggled with that careless comment. When she was finally out in the garden again, she walked slowly toward Baxter's house, mind preoccupied.

Aunt Ella had emphasized one thing clearly, in spite of her faltering speech after the stroke—how happy Gracie had been. That had been the only thing that reconciled her to the sudden marriage that she knew would take Gracie away from her.

Poor Aunt Ella. She'd had no one else. Her parents dead, her only brother killed in Vietnam, leaving his daughter for Ella to raise when his wife drifted off into the hippie subculture. Ella had given all her love to Gracie, and later, to Gracie's daughter,

Now Lydia claimed the love Aunt Ella saw between Gracie and Trey wasn't true—or at least, that her mother's happiness had vanished by the time she arrived in Savannah. What would it have taken them to drive from Wyoming to Savannah? Three days, four? How could all that newlywed joy have been gone already?

"Ms. Grant?" Mrs. Andrews stepped out of the garden door, shading her eyes with one hand. "There was a message for you. Mr. Courtland's secretary called, and they need you to come to their office right away."

She didn't answer until she'd covered the space between them, having no wish to advertise her business to anyone who happened to be around.

"Did he say what he wanted?"

"No, ma'am. Just the secretary, saying please stop by this morning. Do you want me to call a taxi for you?"

"How far away is it?"

"Not that far." Lucas's voice had her spinning around to face him. He stood on the path that led to his house. "I'll walk with you and show you the way."

Another tête-à-tête with Lucas was the last thing she wanted, with the memory of the previous night's emotion fresh in her mind. His face showed no discomfort at all. Had he forgotten so quickly?

"Thanks anyway. I'm sure I can find the office on my own if Mrs. Andrews will give me directions." But Mrs. Andrews had disappeared back into the house, apparently feeling that her duty was done.

"You wouldn't want me to think you don't enjoy my company, would you?" Lucas touched her arm, gesturing toward the gate in the wall that led onto the street. "I'll show you a bit of Savannah while we walk."

Her impulse was to prolong the argument, but that would make his presence into too big a deal. Instead she stepped through the gate and onto the sidewalk, determined to ignore him as much as possible.

Then she paused. "Maybe I should change clothes. I keep forgetting that you people dress a lot more formally than I'm used to."

Lucas's amber gaze slid from her violet challis top to

her white slacks. "You look fine," he said, closing the gate behind them. "What do you think of Savannah so far? Or have you been here before?"

"I've never been east until this trip. All I know comes from the guidebook I read on the plane." They crossed the street to the square. "I did read about the squares, of course."

The city's founder had laid it out around a series of squares, with houses, public buildings and churches grouped around them—quiet oases in the midst of a busy city, the guidebook had said. Now she understood what the book had meant. Tree branches met overhead, and the traffic suddenly seemed faraway. She and Lucas might have been alone in the country.

Lucas gestured toward a row of white brick town houses, each with an intricate wrought-iron railing leading up to a glossy black door. "The wrought iron is characteristic. Kind of reminds you of New Orleans, doesn't it?"

"I wouldn't know." Corrie smiled, realizing they'd embarked on yet another fencing match. "I've never been farther south than St. Louis. As I think I mentioned."

His eyes acknowledged the point. "Savannah is one of the most livable cities in the country and one of the most historic. We aim to keep it that way."

"We?"

"We, as in native Savannahians. You won't find people more devoted to their heritage. It takes quite a few generations to really belong."

A point to him. Obviously she would never belong, any more than her mother had. She thought again of what Lydia had said, realizing she was beginning to feel protective of that young Gracie, as if she were a younger sister instead of her mother.

"You can't walk a step in Savannah without tripping

over history and legend, so mixed up together you can't tell which is which." Lucas had continued his own train of thought. He stopped in front of the monument in the center of the square. "A case in point."

Corrie looked up at the city's founder, James Oglethorpe, sword in hand, cast in bronze.

"Facing the enemy." Lucas's voice was soft in her ear.

"What?" For an instant she thought he meant her, as if the founder of Savannah himself would take a sword to this interloper.

"Oglethorpe. He's facing south, because his enemies were the Spaniards in Florida. What did you think I meant?"

"Nothing." She shouldn't let this get to her. "Thanks for the history lesson."

"Any time, sugar. There's nothing a native enjoys more than talking about his city."

She looked at him, curious at the feeling in his voice. "You sound as if you're in love with it."

"Not it. Her. Savannah is always a female. A faded, genteel Southern lady with just enough eccentricity to make her charming."

Not the place for a forthright Westerner, obviously. Maybe that was why her mother had been unhappy. She'd known from the beginning she'd never belong.

Corrie turned away, and a flight of pigeons took off from the square with a rustle of wings. If she let Lucas make her uncomfortable with every other word, she was in for a very long visit.

"How much farther is it?" Maybe she should have argued a bit more about coming alone. She could have walked along and indulged her own thoughts, instead of being constantly on her guard.

"It's this way." Lucas took her hand as if she were a child who needed guiding. No, not a child, she corrected. There was nothing parental about the way his fingers interlaced with hers. She pulled her hand free.

Lucas smiled. "The office is on Broughton Street. That was the main shopping street of town before the malls wiped it out. It's starting to come back now."

When they'd walked another block to the corner, she saw what he meant. The busy commercial street had a few empty storefronts, but it also boasted the sort of shops usually found in upscale malls. People thronged the sidewalks.

"Is Saturday a big shopping day?" She dodged a large man with a camera who walked backward, focusing.

"Tourists. It's June, and they're out in force. A bus must have just unloaded." He nodded to the crosswalk. "We cross here, and then we should be clear of them. Courtland's office is just down the street."

However, the mob of tourists had apparently decided to go in the same direction, gathering ready to cross as soon as the light changed.

Corrie balanced on the edge of the curb. Even the busy shopping area had its Southern charm, with the gold-embossed plate glass windows of what had probably been old-fashioned department stores now displaying the latest in sportswear.

A bus whizzed by, close enough to the curb to send a blast of hot air in her face. She tried to step back, but people formed a solid mass around her, as if they were afraid they'd never get across the street unless they were first in line.

Annoyed, she turned to look for Lucas. The crowd pushed forward, catching her off balance. She threw out her arms, trying to right herself, just as a shiny sports car accelerated, the driver obviously intent on making it through on the yellow light.

One instant she was safe, her foot hugging the curb. The next a strong shove in her back sent her plunging helplessly into the street, directly into the path of the oncoming car.

FOUR

Adrenaline pumped through Lucas. He plunged past the figures between him and the street. The acrid scent of burning rubber, the shriek of brakes. No time to think, just act. He grabbed Corrie's hand and yanked her out of the street and into his arms.

For an instant longer rational thought evaded him. He held her close, rooted to the pavement. The car rushed by, so close it seemed to touch them, horn blaring as if Corrie, not the driver, had been at fault.

He managed to take a breath. That had been close. Too close. He took a step back from Corrie, his hands still supporting her. "Are you all right?"

Around them the crowd, briefly interested, briefly concerned, moved on. Corrie stared up at him, eyes dark with shock. She shook her head, as if to orient herself, and the shock faded.

"I'm fine." She moved to free herself of his grip, but he held on.

"Not fine. Not yet, anyway. Come over here and sit down for a second." He steered her to a wrought-iron bench in front of an antique shop.

She sank down abruptly, and he suspected her legs were

still shaking. Small wonder. He didn't feel all that well himself, come to think of it. If he'd been a little farther away, he'd never have reached her in time.

The thought sent a surprising wave of anger rushing through him. "Don't they teach you how to cross streets out in the boondocks?"

She just looked at him, her eyes regaining focus. "Someone pushed me."

"Don't be ridiculous." The anger accelerated.

"I'm not." Answering anger brought a flush to her cheeks, chasing away the strain. "I tell you, someone pushed me off the curb."

"The crowd—" he began, but she cut off his words with a scornful look.

"I know the difference between a crowd moving and a hand in the middle of my back." She winced, as if she could still feel it. "Someone put his hand between my shoulder blades and shoved me off the curb."

He wasn't sure what to do with her certainty. On the face of it, the thing seemed impossible. People didn't go around the streets of Savannah shoving total strangers in front of cars.

And then he realized that she was looking at him with suspicion.

"And you think it was me?" In an instant the anger took over again. "I assure you, I don't dislike you that much."

Her eyebrows lifted. "You want to get rid of me."

"You've got me there." The anger vanished, replaced by a small measure of amusement. "But I'd like to see you gone, not dead. I'm neither so stupid nor so impetuous that I'd try a stunt like that."

Corrie frowned at him for a long moment. Then she

nodded. "Okay. I guess I buy that. You're not stupid. And so far I haven't seen anything impetuous about you." She made that sound like a fault.

"Trust me," he said, touching her hand lightly. "My methods are far more orthodox."

For an instant his gaze seemed to tangle with hers. Then she snatched her hand away as if his touch had burned.

She focused on the crowds passing by, her breath still uneven. "Nobody reacted much to my sudden plunge into the street. At home something like that would be a nine days' wonder."

"Savannah is used to eccentrics. If you decided to walk on your hands down the sidewalk, folks would just smile and say good morning."

"Maybe if you did it. Me, I'm an outsider. They'd say I was crazy, not eccentric."

"You may have a point. Shall we put it to the test?" He gestured toward the sidewalk.

Corrie's smile banished the lingering shadow from her eyes. "Not today, thanks. I'd better get on my way to the lawyer's office." She rose.

He stood next to her, hand under her elbow to assure himself that she wasn't going to stumble. "If you'd rather put it off, I'm sure they'd understand."

"Why? Just because somebody tried to push me under a car doesn't mean I'm incapable of walking down the street."

"Do you intend to tell Courtland and Broadbent that?" He frowned down at her, wondering what Baxter's conservative attorneys would make of her claim.

"Not at the moment. After all, I didn't see who pushed me." Her gaze held a challenge.

"I thought we agreed I didn't." He walked beside her to

the corner. If Corrie felt anything when they stopped at the curb, she didn't show it.

The light changed, and they started across the street. She didn't speak until they were safely on the other side. "I agreed you wouldn't try to get rid of me that way." Her tone seemed to reserve judgment on what other ways he might try. "I'm not so sure when it comes to your covering up for someone else."

He'd like to respond with righteous indignation, but he couldn't. He might not be either impetuous or stupid, but he couldn't vouch for Deidre and Ainsley, not the way they'd been behaving lately.

"If you're talking about Deidre and Ainsley, I can assure you I'd have noticed them if they were anywhere near you. They weren't." He kept his voice carefully even.

"I guess I'll have to take your word for that, won't I?"

"Corrie…" He touched her arm, stopping her brisk stride down the sidewalk.

"What?" She swung toward him.

What could he say? She was right—he did want to be rid of her. And he couldn't really trust the behavior of anyone else in the family.

He gestured, pulling the door open for her. "The office is here. I don't suppose you want me to accompany you inside, so I'll wait and walk you home."

"That's not necessary." Her chin came up at the suggestion that she might need an escort.

"Maybe not, but I'm waiting." He smiled at her baffled glare. "Take your time."

She whirled and stalked inside, letting the door bang behind her.

He turned his back on the plate glass window that

showed the outer office of Courtland and Broadbent, surveying the street. Traffic flowed by, tourists thronged. Nothing out of the ordinary.

It had been an accident. What else could it have been? It was ridiculous to go putting familiar faces on lurking dangers. When Corrie came back, he'd do his best to convince her that it had been an accident. The last thing they needed was to have her run to Baxter with tales of assault.

He didn't have to wait long. He heard the door swing and turned. Corrie came down the single step, her expression—what? Curiously blank, that was the closest he could come.

"Corrie? What's wrong?" He took her arm, and his touch seemed to recall her.

She focused on him, frowning. "The lawyers. Neither of them is in today."

"Then why—"

"The receptionist says no one from the office called asking for me. The message was a fake."

"Well, that didn't accomplish much." Corrie frowned at the stout figure of Mrs. Andrews, retreating back to her kitchen domain.

"I'm never sure how much she actually hears." Lucas held the door for her. "Let's go into the garden to talk."

"We don't have anything to talk about. Mrs. Andrews was a dead end, whether she's telling the truth or not."

But she walked into the garden anyway. Lucas's presence was comforting, although the very idea would probably be repugnant to him. He had no desire to be her rescuer, any more than she wanted him to be, but he was.

Lucas waited until she sat at the small table near the roses and then took the chair opposite her. More wrought iron, but green this time instead of black. A faint breeze ruffled the roses, sending their rich scent through the air.

"I can't see any reason why Mrs. Andrews would lie about the call," he said.

Corrie lifted her eyebrows. She wasn't quite as accepting of the woman's motives as Lucas seemed to be. But then, he might have a good reason to pretend to believe her.

"Would she lie if Deidre told her to? Or if it was Deidre's voice on the phone?"

Lucas's face tightened, lines deepening around his eyes. "Why do you have it in for Deidre? Just because Mrs. Andrews said it was a woman on the phone, that doesn't mean it was she."

"Deidre has been pretty open about her feelings. Maybe you think she wouldn't do anything rash, but I'm not so sure."

"That's ridiculous. Anyway, I'd have noticed Deidre in the crowd." He glared at her as if she were to blame. "I'm telling you, she wasn't there."

Her temper flared at his stubbornness. "Somebody set me up. Why not Deidre?"

"This could have been just coincidence." But his expression said he didn't believe that himself.

"Right." She let the contempt in her voice say it all. "If not Deidre…" A chill brushed her spine. "Mrs. Andrews would say anything her employer told her to, wouldn't she?"

"Baxter? That's even more ridiculous. Baxter's the one who brought you here. Why would he want to get rid of you?"

"I can't imagine. But then, I haven't been able to understand why he does anything."

She thought of the story Lydia had told, about the portrait of Trey. A man who would try to destroy the only thing he had left of his dead son would do anything. The chill intensified in spite of the warm, humid air. No, she was wrong. The portrait hadn't been the only thing left of his dead son. She was.

"Baxter may be autocratic." Lucas's frown deepened. Was he thinking of something specific? "But he never acts irrationally."

"Unless you agree with Deidre that he was irrational to bring me here."

He shook his head slowly. "I don't understand it, but that doesn't mean he doesn't have a good reason."

She shrugged. "I wouldn't know about that. But if you eliminate Deidre and Mr. Manning from planning today's little accident, the pool of candidates is pretty small."

She watched his expression as he tried to cope with that. He didn't like it, but she'd figured out by now that Lucas had a certain innate honesty. That honesty wouldn't let him pretend, however much he might want to, that she was wrong.

Poor Lucas. He didn't want to be allied to her in any way, but he also couldn't connive at violence. That left him in the unenviable position of trying to protect her and defend his family at the same time.

"Daddy!" Jason plunged out of a dense clump of azaleas and darted toward his father. "I didn't know you were home yet. Hi, Cousin Corrie."

Lucas's face softened at the sight of his son. He put his arm around the boy and drew him close. "What are you doing out here? Aren't you supposed to be with your grandmother?"

Jason frowned, looking for a moment very like his father. "I guess."

"Why aren't you?"

For a moment longer the child pouted, and she had a

sense of strong emotions withheld. Then the words seemed to burst out of him. "Grandma never lets me do anything! She just wants me to sit and work puzzles and read story-books. That's no fun."

Lucas brushed fine blond hair back from his son's forehead. "I thought you liked puzzles. Grandma got you that new dinosaur puzzle, remember?"

"I know. But I already worked it, and I wanted to play cowboys in the garden." He flashed a glance toward Corrie. "Cousin Corrie understands. She's a cowgirl."

She shook her head, smiling, not willing to be drawn into their dispute. "Only once in a while. Most of the time I wait tables."

"I want to learn to ride. Please, Daddy."

Lucas looked troubled, and she wondered what really lay behind this apparent dispute over what Jason could do. "Grandma thinks it's not a good idea."

"Just 'cause I have asthma, she doesn't want me to have any fun."

"Jason, you know that's not true. Grandma loves you very much."

Judging by Jason's mutinous expression, he'd probably like to be loved a little less at this point. So the boy was asthmatic. That explained Eulalie's protectiveness, she supposed. Still, she'd taught youngsters in class who had asthma, and they'd been able to lead fairly normal lives.

"Jason, there you are!" Eulalie hustled toward them, her clouded expression clearing when she saw the boy. "That was very naughty, to come outside without telling me. I thought you were taking a nap."

"I don't need a nap. I'm not a baby. I don't, do I, Daddy?"

Lucas looked harassed on all sides. "No, of course you

don't need a nap." He shot an annoyed look at Eulalie. "But you shouldn't have come outside without asking your grandmother."

"She'd just have said no."

"That's not the point." Lucas turned his son toward Eulalie. "Tell Grandma you're sorry, and then go on in the house."

Jason stared at the brick walkway for a moment. Then he looked up at his grandmother. "I'm sorry, Grandma." He spun and ran toward the house.

"Jason, don't run…" Eulalie called.

"Leave the boy alone." Lucas's words probably came out with more force than he'd intended. He softened them with a smile. "He'll be fine. Thank you for watching him."

Eulalie's soft mouth took on a surprising firmness. "He won't be fine if he rushes all over the place and has an attack." She turned a fierce glare on Corrie. "All he can talk about is riding since he met you. I'll thank you to leave him alone."

Before Corrie could find any words in defense, Eulalie had bustled off in Jason's wake.

Obviously Eulalie wasn't the marshmallow Corrie had imagined. On the subject of her grandson, at least, she had strong feelings she didn't mind voicing.

"I'm sorry about that." Lucas sounded strained. He probably hated the fact that that little scene had played out in front of her. "Jason dislikes having his grandmother hover over him, even when it's necessary."

"Is it necessary? I'm no expert on children with asthma, but—"

"You're right." His mouth narrowed to a thin line. "You're not an expert, and I'd appreciate it if you kept your opinions to yourself." He turned and stalked away, leaving her staring after him.

This seemed to be her day for making people hate her. Not that she'd had to work very hard at that lately. And obviously the faint bond she'd imagined between herself and Lucas was just that—imagination.

Corrie waited on the sidewalk the next morning, feeling something less than her usual Sunday-morning anticipation. She'd had every intention of seeking out a church service on her own, but Eulalie had simply assumed she'd attend church with the family. So here she was, feeling about ten again as Eulalie surveyed her navy suit and then gave a satisfied nod. Apparently she'd pass.

Two cars pulled to the curb—the town car, with Jefferson at the wheel, then Lucas, driving what she supposed was his own sedan. Corrie hesitated, unsure which car to get in, while Eulalie and Deidre slid into the town car.

Ainsley held the door, flushing a little. "I'll sit up front with the driver, Corrie."

But Lucas took her arm. "Corrie will ride with us. We'll meet you there."

She slid into the front seat, glancing at him as he got behind the wheel. "Trying to keep me out of trouble?"

"Let's say I think riding with us will be more conducive to a spiritual frame of mind."

"For me or for Deidre?"

"For both of you."

In actual fact, they probably could have walked to the church just as easily. Two squares over, two streets down—she was beginning to have a map of Savannah in her mind, the historic district, at any rate. It wasn't large, as cities went. The squares gave the effect of a giant checkerboard to the old part of the city, where the family seemed to spend most of its time.

"Parking is always a challenge," Lucas said. "Jason, are you keeping your eyes open?"

"I sure am." Jason bounced a little in the backseat, as if he wanted to be the one to find a parking space.

"The church doesn't have its own lot?" She was still trying to get used to the confined spaces of the old city, still feeling a bit claustrophobic now and then as it seemed to close in on her.

"It does, but the lot is the size of a postage stamp. Oglethorpe didn't foresee motor vehicles when he laid out his city, and the churches and public buildings are stuck on their trust lots."

Seeing her blank expression, he smiled. "Trust lots. The squares were designed with lots for churches, libraries and other public buildings on the east and west sides of the squares. The north and south sides of the squares were designated for residences."

"Another tradition, I gather."

"You can't take a step in Savannah without tripping over a tradition of some sort."

"This is a nice one, though. It adds a kind of orderliness to public life—recognizing the role of the church."

"Yes, it does." The look he sent her was—a little surprised, perhaps. Maybe he'd thought the church would be foreign territory to her. After all, he did see her as a con artist. She shouldn't forget that.

"There's one, Daddy." Jason threatened to bounce out of his seat belt in his excitement. "Grab it quick."

"Good going, Jase." Lucas backed effortlessly into the small space. "This is as close as we ever get."

It felt odd, walking the half block to the church with Lucas and Jason. The boy skipped between them, obviously considering himself far too old to hold hands. To a casual observer they might look like a family, dressed in their Sunday best. No observer could guess, from his smiling expression, what Lucas really thought of her.

The church, like so many of the houses, had the characteristic curving double staircase leading up to what must be the sanctuary on the second floor. The building wore an air of grace and permanence, looking out onto the leafy, green square that Oglethorpe had laid out for his city.

The church clearly predated anything one might find in Ulee. As they approached the three people who stood waiting for them at the base of the stairs, she had the sense that everything here guarded itself behind that tradition Lucas had spoken of.

"Built in the early 1800s," Lucas said, as if she'd asked a question. "The Mannings and the Santees have been attending here for about that long."

Deidre, hearing what he said, smiled. "That's Savannah," she said. "You can't belong unless you've been here a century or so."

Corrie stiffened. That barbed comment was meant for her, obviously.

"In that case I have an advantage, don't I?" She smiled sweetly. "Since my father's family has been here at least that long."

Deidre looked as if she'd like to say several things that would be inappropriate on the very steps of the church.

"Let's go in," Eulalie said quickly, maybe fearing her daughter's temper would get the better of her discretion.

They started up the stairs, with Ainsley, Jason and Lucas

hanging back to let the women precede them. As Corrie passed Lucas, she caught a look that might almost be admiration on his face.

For her? No, she couldn't believe that.

In spite of her brave words, her nerves danced as she followed Eulalie through the double doors. She was about to face a number of people who probably remembered her father—who would, perhaps, be looking at her and judging her.

A wide center aisle swept graciously forward between ranks of curving white pews. On either side wall, venerable stained glass windows depicted stories from both Old and New Testament.

Eulalie went quickly down the aisle, nodding to people on either side but not stopping. Because she didn't want to have to introduce Corrie? Perhaps.

At the third row from the front, Eulalie slid into the pew on the right. A family pew, probably, from the way she had gone unerringly to it. Corrie slipped in after her.

After a bit of juggling, Jason managed to get past his father and settle down next to her on the cushioned pew. Corrie smiled at him, her heart warmed by his acceptance. Someone here liked her, even if it was for her cowgirl status in his eyes.

She'd expected to find attending the service here difficult, but once the worship began, she was swept into it. The setting might be different from the tiny church in Ulee, and the form a bit strange, but the sweet spirit that filled the sanctuary was the same.

She relaxed, opening her heart to worship.

When the service ended, the introductions she'd dreaded began, but it was Lucas who made most of them, merely saying she was visiting from Wyoming. Warmed by the service, she found it fairly easy to nod, smile and ignore the pointed glances aimed at her. It was all right. It didn't matter what they thought, only that she'd worshipped this day.

They were back on the sidewalk before she looked around and realized that one thing she'd expected, one thing she'd hoped for, wasn't here.

"Looking for something?" Lucas paused next to her.

She shook her head. "Not really. I just thought the church might have a cemetery next to it. I should have realized that wouldn't be the case right in the city."

"A cemetery?" he echoed.

She lifted her chin, preparing for the reaction she'd undoubtedly receive. "I'd like to see my father's grave."

She heard a sharp intake of breath behind her. Eulalie's face crumpled slightly, as if she were about to cry. Deidre elbowed her way past her mother.

"I'll take you to the cemetery." Her smile had an edge as sharp as a knife.

Lucas took Corrie's elbow in a grip of iron. "That won't be necessary. Jason and I will take her."

He piloted Corrie away from the others so abruptly that she nearly stumbled. There was no longer any question about it in her mind—he wanted to keep her away from Deidre. For whose sake, she wondered. Deidre's? Or hers?

FIVE

Had he been too obvious? Lucas wasn't sure. He negotiated the after-church traffic with half his attention, threading his way toward Liberty Street. He wasn't sure what was going through Deidre's mind now. Once she'd confided in him, looking on him as a big brother, but those days were long gone.

He didn't believe Deidre had anything to do with Corrie's accident—of course he didn't. He'd just thought it a bad idea for her to escort Corrie to Bonaventure Cemetery and the family graves.

From the backseat, Jason was serving as tour guide, pointing out the horse-drawn carriage tour as it clip-clopped past them.

"The horses know their route even better than the drivers do, Cousin Corrie. Did you know that?"

"No, but I'm not surprised. I led horseback tours one summer, and our horses did, too. They didn't like it if I tried to take an alternate route."

Corrie sat half-turned in her seat, looking back at his son. Sunlight coming through the windshield brought out the freckles on her cheeks and gilded her smooth skin.

Enough, he reminded himself. You cannot be attracted to her, no matter who she is.

And if she really was Trey's daughter? The question was there, however much he might deny it. What would happen then?

"I'll bet that was fun." Jason's mind was clearly still on the horses. "I'd like to do that someday."

"You're already a good tour guide," Corrie said. "You know more about Savannah than I do."

"He should." Lucas smiled wryly. "I'm afraid he's had it drummed into him from birth. Jason, tell Corrie about Bonaventure Cemetery."

"That's where all our kin are buried, but there's lots of famous people there, too."

"And plenty of tourists since the publication of a certain book." He grimaced. "I hope it won't be too bad at this hour. The statuary is worth seeing, even if you don't have relatives there."

Corrie's eyebrows lifted. "Meaning I'm only going as a tourist?"

He had no particular desire to enter into an argument about her identity at the moment. "Meaning it's worth going as a tourist, that's all. Don't try to start a fight with me, Corrie. I don't fight on the Sabbath."

"Fine." She looked away from the challenge in his gaze. "Give me your best tourist spiel, then."

"This section of town is called Thunderbolt." He merged onto Bonaventure Road, glad to leave some of the traffic behind. "The cemetery site was a plantation once—it didn't become a cemetery until the 1800s. Before that, burials were in Colonial Park Cemetery, right in the city." He made the turn between the cemetery gates. "And here we are."

He parked, getting out slowly. Jason, already out of the car, trotted immediately toward the family graves. Fortunately his son didn't have the mixed feelings he did about this place.

He glanced at Corrie as she fell into step with him. She didn't look as if she were concentrating on the moss-draped live oaks or the view of the river.

"Why didn't you want Deidre to bring me here?"

Her question caught him off guard, but he managed a smile. "Wouldn't you rather be here with two charming gentlemen?"

"That's not the point. I want to know why—"

"Yes, I get the picture." Obviously charm wasn't going to work. "Can't we just leave it that I wasn't eager for the two of you to get into a wrangle over the family graves?"

"I don't wrangle." Her eyes flashed.

"Maybe not, but Deidre does."

She didn't answer for a moment. The cemetery was very still—they'd obviously gotten here before the tour groups. A mockingbird sang, then swooped away when Jason got too close to its tree.

"Someone searched my room," Corrie said abruptly.

He stopped dead. "What are you talking about?"

"My room. In Baxter's house. Someone searched through my things."

"That's impossible." But he knew it wasn't. Actually, searching Corrie's room probably made a great deal of rather skewed sense to someone like Deidre, or possibly even Eulalie.

"Is it?" Her eyebrows lifted, and the look she gave him said that she knew what he was thinking. "You're not going to tell me Deidre would balk at that, if she thought she'd find something to discredit me."

"Did she?" He shot the question at her.

She shook her head, smiling a little. "She couldn't, because there isn't anything." The smile faded. "But she— or whoever did it—took something."

This was worse than he'd thought. He could imagine Baxter's reaction. "What's missing?"

"Some notes that I made about the family. The attorneys filled me in on all of you before I left Wyoming."

He began walking again, mind busy with possibilities. It would be best if Corrie could be persuaded that she was wrong.

"Why would anyone take that?"

She fell into step with him. "I haven't a clue. The notes were hardly incriminating."

"Look, Corrie, I can understand why you might jump to the conclusion that someone searched your room, but that doesn't make any sense, now does it?"

She shook her head slowly, as if reluctant to give up her theory.

"What probably happened was that the paper blew off onto the floor. You don't know Mrs. Andrews like I do. She's a fierce cleaner—you don't dare put down a newspaper you haven't finished reading or it'll be in the recycling bin. She probably threw the notes away, that's all."

"I suppose." But she didn't sound convinced.

"So what did Baxter's attorneys have to say about us?" He kept his voice light, but he didn't like it—the idea that they'd passed on information about the family. About him.

"Just some general facts, so I'd know who to expect when I got here." Her smile flickered. "You were described as an award-winning architect."

"A bit fulsome, but true, I suppose."

"Actually, I looked you up on the Internet. If anything, they understated the case. It did make me wonder, though."

"Wonder what?"

"Why you're running Baxter's companies instead of your own architecture firm."

A good question. Too bad he didn't have a good answer. Corrie had a way of striking right to the heart of the matter.

Because I can't go out on my own. Because I'm tied hand and foot by tradition, responsibility, duty. But he wouldn't say any of those things to Corrie.

"I'm satisfied with what I'm doing." He stopped at the low concrete wall that had replaced rusting wrought-iron fences fifty years earlier. "Here are the Santees—most of them, anyway."

"Your family." She looked a little startled. "I didn't realize—of course if I'd thought, I'd have realized your family plot would be here, too. Savannah aristocrats, like the Mannings."

Was that really how she saw them? "That sort of thing doesn't mean anything now." If anything, it was a weight, keeping them from doing what they wanted with their lives.

Jason walked toward them on the wall, hands out for balance. He hopped down. "That's my mama's stone." He pointed for Corrie's benefit. "She's in Heaven with Jesus, you know."

"Yes, I know." Corrie's voice softened. "Did you help plant those pretty flowers?"

Jason nodded and bent to touch the purple geraniums. "Daddy says purple was Mama's favorite color. I don't remember."

Lucas gritted his teeth to keep from snapping that Jason should remember. Why should he? He was a child—his memories were fading. Any that he still had were bound to be of his mother pale and weak, propped up on a hospital bed.

"It was nice that you planted purple ones then," Corrie said. Her gaze moved from stone to stone—Santees dating back to the earliest burials in Bonaventure. Her expression didn't tell him what she was thinking. That they worshipped the past here? He sometimes thought that himself.

He turned, walking to the Manning enclosure, sheltered under the branches of one of the towering live oaks. "And here are the Manning graves." He stopped at the most recent markers. "Baxter's wife. And Trey."

Corrie came to a halt beside him. She bent over Trey's stone, her hair swinging forward to hide her face, reading the inscription. Baxter James Manning, III, 1953–1975. No verse. Baxter had been too angry, so Lucas's mother had said, to bother with the finer points. Finally Corrie straightened.

He studied her expression, not knowing quite what to make of it. "Satisfied?"

"No." She swallowed, the muscles in her neck working. "I thought when I saw it, I'd feel…I don't know. Sad, maybe, or angry."

"What do you feel?"

"Nothing." She looked up at him, her forehead puckering. "I don't feel anything at all."

"I'm not sure what I've accomplished since I got here." Corrie leaned back in the chintz-upholstered chair of her bedroom the next afternoon, cell phone cradled against her ear.

Ann was the only person she could really talk to. With everyone here she had to be on guard.

"It's not like you to let yourself get down." Ann's voice

was warm and concerned. "Stop and think about it. Why did you go to Savannah?"

Corrie frowned at the needlework hassock under her feet—needlework done by some Manning ancestor, she supposed. "To find out who I am. What I came from. To understand my father."

To know what happened to her father and mother. Wasn't that really the question in her mind? What could have been strong enough to damage their love so quickly?

"Okay, so who would know about your father?"

"Baxter. Eulalie. Lydia. Probably other friends I haven't met yet."

"Well then, that's who you should be talking to. Nobody can stop you from asking questions."

She thought of Eulalie's anger when she'd felt Corrie was interfering in family matters. Of Lydia's brittle criticisms.

"They don't have to answer."

"Doesn't mean you shouldn't ask. Come on, Corrie. This isn't like you. You know what you want and go after it, you don't sit around feeling sorry for yourself."

"Ouch."

"You deserve it." She could hear Ann's grin through the phone. "Get off your tail feathers, cowgirl, and go after them."

"All right, all right," she capitulated, laughing. "I guess that was what I needed—a little home-brewed plain talk. Thanks, Annie."

"Anytime." Ann hesitated. "You know, I was going to give you a call if you hadn't phoned today."

"Why? Did the fuses blow again?" The café's aging wiring had to be replaced, but the money for that had gone for hospital bills.

Ann sniffed. "I wouldn't call you for something I can

handle. Fact is, someone's been wandering around town, asking questions about you."

She shot off the chair, fingers tightening on the phone. "Who is it?"

"My guess is a private investigator." The laughter was back in Ann's voice. "He tried to pump Luis. Offered him twenty bucks to talk about you. He's lucky Luis didn't knock him down."

She wouldn't put it past her seventy-year-old handyman to tackle someone half his age and twice his size. "Tell Luis to behave himself."

"You don't sound surprised."

No, she didn't. "I hadn't thought about it, but I guess it was inevitable. Someone would be bound to check up on me."

"Well, don't let them get you down, sweetie. You know we're all praying for you."

"I know." She would not let her voice choke with tears. "Thanks, Annie. I'll talk to you again soon."

She stood, staring at the phone for a moment after she'd ended the call. Lucas. It had to be Lucas. Hiring a private investigator was exactly what he'd do.

That fact shouldn't hurt as much as it seemed to. Lucas had never made any secret of his opinion of her.

Those moments when she'd felt he was accepting her had been illusion. Even at the cemetery, where Lucas had seemed to soften, he hadn't really offered any sympathy, maybe because he didn't believe she stood at her father's grave. He hadn't asked about her mother's grave. If he had, what would she have told him? That she had drowned, her body never found? That would lead to secrets she didn't intend to share. She had no friends in Savannah—only people who'd get rid of her the first chance they got.

Lucas would be disappointed in his private investigator's report. She was exactly who she said she was, and nobody in Ulee would tell him anything else. If they talked to him at all, that was. Folks in Ulee took care of their own. Luis wasn't the only one who'd happily take a swing at the investigator if he got too inquisitive.

She was unaccountably cheered at the thought. Ann was right. Sitting around feeling sorry for herself accomplished nothing. The person who'd decoyed her to the lawyer's office and shoved her off the curb probably thought she was too frightened to do anything.

Well, she wasn't. She'd go after what she wanted, and she'd start with Eulalie. Grabbing her bag, she went quickly down the stairs and out into the garden.

Someone came out of Eulalie's garden door just as she reached it. Deidre. Corrie braced herself for the inevitable verbal sniping that seemed to be Deidre's second nature.

"I'm looking for your mother. Is she at home?"

To her surprise, Deidre actually managed a smile. "I'm afraid not. She's having dinner with friends."

"I'll see her tomorrow, then." It was a bit deflating to be all charged up to do something, only to find the opportunity vanished.

Deidre watched her for a moment, eyes slightly narrowed, and then seemed to reach a decision. "I'm on my way to the shop to work for a couple of hours. Why don't you ride along with me? River Street is worth exploring, and we can meet when I get off work for a late supper."

The invitation was so startling that Corrie could only gape at her for a moment. What had gotten into Deidre? "Are you serious?"

"You don't need to sound so surprised."

"Sure I do. You haven't had a kind word for me since I got here, and now you're inviting me out." To say nothing of the fact that I think you may be the one playing dirty tricks on me.

"Maybe I just decided to listen to my mother's advice on how to be a Southern lady." Deidre's gaze evaded hers.

"Somehow I doubt that."

Deidre shrugged. "Suit yourself. I just thought you might want to do something other than sit around here."

The words stung, because they were an unconscious echo of what Ann had said. But Ann had her best interests at heart, while Deidre—

But what difference did that make? And if Deidre was setting her up for another unpleasant little episode? Well, if so, Deidre would discover she had more than met her match.

Besides, Lucas had been eager to keep her away from Deidre. That in itself seemed a good reason to take her up on the offer.

"Fine. Thanks. I'd like to."

"Good." Deidre nodded and gestured toward the gate in the wall. "My car's on the street. This way."

For an instant Corrie's back seemed to tingle with the memory of being pushed into the street. But that couldn't have been Deidre. She couldn't have missed seeing her, if she'd been in that crowd. Deidre might be unpleasant, but she knew more about the family than Corrie ever would. That was worth a bit of unpleasantness. She followed Deidre out of the gate.

Corrie glanced up toward the gold dome of City Hall, soaring over River Street. According to the clock, she had about ten minutes until her meeting with Deidre, so she'd better leave the shops behind and head back up.

Up was certainly the operative word. River Street, obviously, ran along the river, but immediately behind the shops and restaurants that had been cleverly tucked into the old cotton warehouses, the bluff on which Savannah was built rose sharply. To get from one level to the other, you climbed.

She picked her way carefully over the cobblestone car ramp toward the stairs she'd come down. Ballast stones, according to the brochure she'd picked up before she'd started exploring. Impossible, to think the stones she stepped on had come over on the earliest sailing ships. Not easy walking—fortunately she'd had sturdy sandals on when she'd left the house so impulsively.

The antique shop where Deidre worked was on Factor's Walk, an odd little walkway halfway up the bluff. She started up the steep stone steps, clutching the metal railing. They'd been treacherous enough in daylight, and now that it was getting dark, shadows lay deeply across them.

She reached the walkway that led to Deidre's shop, and her steps quickened. For the first time, she looked forward to talking with Deidre. Prickly as she was, maybe she'd begun to accept the fact that Corrie didn't represent a threat. Although Deidre wouldn't remember Trcy, she'd certainly have heard plenty of family stories.

A feather of unease touched her as she made her way along the walkway that had been crowded with shoppers earlier. Now the shops whose doors had been open to welcome visitors were dark and shuttered for the most part. Well, perhaps Deidre's shop stayed open later than its neighbors.

It didn't. She stopped, staring blankly in the darkened

windows, and then checked her watch. She was on time. Where was Deidre?

She rapped on the door, telling herself that Deidre might still be inside, but she didn't really believe it. The shop was empty—Deidre was gone.

She tried to shrug off the suspicion that gripped her. Deidre might have left work early and gone on to where the car was parked.

She hurried back along the walkway, wondering why the city fathers hadn't seen fit to put a few more lampposts in this dark stretch, and on up the stairs to Bay Street. She remembered where Deidre had parked—go through the small park, past the cannons, down half a block—

The car was gone. The excuses she'd been making for Deidre's nonappearance were just that, excuses. Anger boiled up. That was absolutely the last time she trusted any of these people. They were nothing but a bunch of hypocrites, acting as if they were friendly and scheming behind her back.

She stopped in midrant.

Sorry, Father. I suppose Deidre thinks she has good reasons for acting the way she has been. I'm having trouble turning the other cheek. That was certainly an understatement. *I guess You've noticed that. If this weren't so important, I'd head back to where I belong.*

Would she go back? Maybe not, because the simple truth was that she didn't know where she belonged any longer. That was what she was here to find out, so she'd have to take the bad with the good until she found the answers she needed. The bad, in this case, included Cousin Deidre.

Well, her immediate need was to get back to the house. The taxis that had been so plentiful earlier had vanished. She could call the house, ask for someone to pick her up, but that would mean admitting that she'd fallen for Deidre's little trick.

She could walk. It wasn't that far, and at least Savannah's geography was fairly easy to master. Streets ran parallel to the river or at right angles to it, and the squares made easy-to-find markers. The route between Factor's Row and the house was fairly obvious. She crossed Bay Street and started down the side street that would bring her out a few blocks from the square.

Once she was away from the lights and traffic of Bay Street, the sidewalks were surprisingly empty. Apparently the tourists had all either found restaurants open for a late dinner or were back at their hotels, resting their feet after walking all day.

Raucous noise and music spilled from a club on the opposite side of the street. She kept walking. In the next block, dense hedges lined the street, hiding the houses behind them and crowding onto the sidewalk. She was halfway to the corner when she realized she was no longer alone. Footsteps came along the sidewalk behind her.

Automatically she sped up. The echoing footsteps came faster, as well, as if the person behind were keeping time with the rhythm of her pace. Apprehension slid along her skin like a touch, and she shrugged it away. Why shouldn't someone else walk along the same street she did? And if it was Deidre, intent on some mischief, she'd get more than she bargained for.

She stopped, intending to pull her cell phone from her bag. The other footsteps stopped, too.

Her heartbeat jolted. That was stretching coincidence a little too far for comfort. Why wasn't there someone around? She'd have gone to a stranger's door, but the houses, safe behind their hedges and gates, weren't welcoming. Somehow it would be worse to pull at a locked gate, betraying her panic to the person behind her.

Panic? A welcoming flood of anger coursed through her. She would not allow these people to panic her. If this was Deidre's idea of a joke…

She stopped, turned, fueled by anger. Even as she spun around she glimpsed movement. A dark shadow, too tall and bulky to be Deidre, pressed back into the denser shadow of the hedge.

Her breath caught. No casual pedestrian would behave that way. Whether it was an anonymous mugger or someone who posed a personal threat, there was nothing innocent about that sudden evasion.

Heart pounding, she spun and hurried toward the corner, lit by its streetlamps. If she could reach that welcoming pool of light, she'd feel safe.

But the footsteps behind her came in a rush, and she responded instinctively, without taking the time to think. She darted into the empty street. She'd have to run for it, have to hope someone would come—

A car swung around the corner, its headlights catching her. It seemed to accelerate, and she was frozen between two dangers, not knowing which way to run.

Then the car pulled to a stop beside her, and the driver leaned across to open the passenger door. It was Lucas.

SIX

Lucas wasn't sure whether he was more annoyed with Deidre or with Corrie. "What were you doing out in the street?"

"Nothing." She snapped the seat belt around her, her gaze evading his. "Thanks for the lift."

"Anytime." He studied her for a moment. Something was clearly wrong—he could see that in the tenseness of her shoulders and the way she looked anywhere but at him. Just as clearly, she didn't intend to tell him.

She turned toward him, mustering a smile. If he hadn't seen that momentary stress, he might have bought it. "How did you happen to be here just in time to give me a ride?"

He considered making up some excuse, but he was tired of dancing around subjects with her, and equally tired of trying to defend the indefensible.

"I was there when Deidre came home. I could tell by her attitude that something was up. She looked exactly the way she used to when she'd gotten into trouble at school."

Corrie blinked at his bluntness. "Did she tell you what happened?"

"She said that you were supposed to meet her for a ride home, but you didn't show up, so she left without you." His fingers tightened on the steering wheel, and he forced them to relax. There was no point in overreacting. "I didn't think you should walk back alone."

"Overprotective?" Her eyebrows lifted. "How did you find me?"

"If you were walking you'd obviously come down one of two or three streets from Bay. I've been cruising them." Looking. Worrying.

"Thank you."

He glanced toward her but could read nothing in her face. "So what really happened?"

"Deidre suggested I explore River Street while she put in a couple of hours at the shop. We were supposed to meet and go out for a late supper. I was there on time, but she'd already left."

"I'm sorry." He hadn't done it, but he still felt the need to apologize.

"It's not your fault. I should have known Deidre's friendliness was too good to be true."

The words sounded lonelier than she probably meant them to. With a spurt of recklessness, he pulled into a U-turn, heading back toward the waterfront.

Corrie gripped the armrest. "What are you doing?"

"You were promised supper, weren't you?"

"You don't have to do that."

"I know I don't. I want to." To his surprise, he realized that was true.

He'd take Corrie to a restaurant—they'd sit and talk. Maybe he'd get a little more insight into who she was and what she wanted. And if not? The experience still might be enjoyable.

He kept the conversation safely on Savannah's nightlife

as he drove down to River Street, where he found a parking space in one of the small lots along the river.

"Never park here when we're getting one of our frog-choking downpours," he said, getting out. "Unless you want to wade through knee-deep water when you come back to your car."

Corrie joined him, glancing up at the star-encrusted sky. "No chance of that tonight, I'd think."

"No." He touched her arm, and she fell into step beside him. "No storms tonight."

He hoped. Corrie seemed remarkably calm. Maybe in Ulee it was considered safe for a woman to walk alone after dark. Or maybe, as she'd said, he was being overprotective.

"This is nice." She gestured toward the brick sidewalks illuminated by old-fashioned lampposts, lined by shops and restaurants along the bluff side. The river slid darkly past on their left.

"It is, isn't it? I hope you had a chance to explore."

She nodded. "I even bought a few souvenirs for the folks back home."

"Nothing emblazoned 'Yankee, go home,' I hope."

"I managed to resist, but the clerk told me they sell very well. To Northerners. I didn't quite understand all the shamrocks, though. I thought I was in Georgia, not Ireland."

"St. Patrick's Day is huge here—nobody quite knows why. It's second only to the Georgia-Florida football game in importance to Savannahians. And it's harder to avoid. Think Mardi Gras in green, and you have the right image." He steered her into his favorite restaurant, nodding to the hostess. "For now you'll have to indulge another favorite Savannah habit—good food."

She followed the hostess to a table, looking appreciatively at the dark wooden beams that crossed the low ceiling and the prints of sailing ships gracing the white-washed walls. "Very nice. Is it really old, or just meant to look that way?"

"Bite your tongue." He held her chair while she slid into it. "Savannah doesn't need pretence. These buildings along the riverfront were cotton warehouses a couple of centuries ago."

"I guess I did read that in one of the brochures I picked up."

"Did you walk all the way down to the waving girl?" If she'd seen the statue of the girl waving to passing ships, supposedly waiting for her beloved to return, she'd have noticed it.

Corrie nodded.

"Do I sense a certain lack of enthusiasm for the sights?"

She shrugged. "I didn't come here to play tourist, beautiful as the city is. I came to find out about my father." Her gaze met his, suddenly challenging. "Don't I have the right to do that?"

The server came just then, saving him from a reply he didn't want to make. They ordered—the crab soup for him, a Reuben sandwich for Corrie—and he insisted she try a side order of sweet potato fries.

When the server had moved away again, he knew he had to answer. No one else sat near them, and he couldn't find a reason to avoid the question.

"If you're really Trey's daughter, you have a right to all the answers you want, I suppose."

Her eyes flashed. "Hasn't your private investigator assured you of my identity yet? I'm surprised at him. Maybe you should try someone else."

That jolted him. He'd assumed the investigator would be discreet. "How did you find out?"

"Believe it or not, I do have friends. And in a town of 569, everyone notices a stranger."

He should have realized that. "He confirmed that you're Corrie Jane Grant. That your mother was Grace Grant, who died when you were six months old. That you were raised by an elderly aunt, now deceased, who had also raised your mother after her father was killed in Vietnam."

"Very efficient. I could have told you all that."

"You're Grace's daughter. No one's questioning that. It doesn't necessarily mean that you're Trey's child."

Color came up in her cheeks at that. "I'm sure your investigator confirmed the date of my birth. Do the math. Unless my mother was having an affair with someone else within a few months of her wedding—" She stopped, shaking her head. "I can't prove anything about my mother, I suppose. She's only a faded photo to me. But my aunt told me, and she wasn't lying, any more than I am."

He was swayed by her passion. How could he help it? But he had to be careful with her. "You have lied, Corrie."

Her eyes widened. "What are you talking about?"

"You let us think you were a waitress, when you're really an elementary physical education teacher. Isn't that a lie?"

Her lips twitched. "I never said that. Anyway, no one asked. You were all so obvious about your contempt for me. Why should I bother correcting you? And there's nothing wrong with being a server, is there?"

He couldn't argue without sounding like a snob. "That isn't the point. You wanted us to think you were an uneducated hick."

"No, that's what you wanted to believe." Amusement

crinkled her eyes. "Admit it. I can imagine the conversations that went on before I arrived."

She had him there, and he raised his hands in surrender. "All right, I confess. Maybe I do owe you an apology for that."

"I don't want an apology," she said. "I want you to tell me about Trey."

He'd reached just the point he'd been avoiding. He studied her face for a moment, as the server put dishes down in front of them and moved away.

Did it really matter whether she was Trey's daughter or not? Even if she wasn't, telling her what he remembered about Trey wouldn't help or hurt in any way that he could see.

"What do you want to know?" he said finally.

For an instant she looked like a kid anticipating Christmas morning. "Whatever you remember about him." She paused. "That's all I want. I know none of you believe that, but it's true. I always thought I'd never know who my father was. I thought that blank line on my birth certificate would haunt me forever. Now—I just want to understand."

He tried to put himself in her place, but he couldn't. He'd always known who his people were—that was the most important thing in the South, after all. He'd always felt both the pride and the burden of all those generations of Santees.

"Trey was always a part of my life—our families were as close as two families could be. Related, too, somewhere back along the family tree. But it's odd to think how little I really know personally."

"He was quite a bit older than you."

He nodded. "I have only a few vague memories of Trey

from when I visited the house as a child. He was grown then—he didn't take any interest in me, other than to dispense a little of the charm that drew people to him."

He has too much careless charm, Lucas's mother had always said about Trey. She'd thought that could be a dangerous thing.

"Maybe that was what attracted my mother." Corrie sounded as if she agreed with his mother.

"Maybe." He dug into memory, trying to find something that would satisfy her. "My parents always felt Baxter spoiled him, I know. He was the golden boy, the child who was going to inherit everything Baxter had built up." He shrugged. "I suppose all those expectations got to be too much after a while. Trey wanted to go his own way, and Baxter didn't like it."

"Lydia said they fought all the time. She thinks marrying my mother was just part of some grand rebellion against his father."

That sounded rather blunt, even for Lydia. "Trey and Baxter loved each other, I'm sure. If they'd had more time, they'd have made it up."

"But they didn't have time." She stared down at her half-eaten sandwich, then pushed it away from her. "Will you tell me how he died?"

"You mean you don't know?"

"Who would tell me?"

That was unanswerable. He felt a stirring of pity for Corrie. Whatever her motives had been in contacting Baxter, if she was Trey's child, she'd been shortchanged when it came to family.

"It was a freak accident." He tried to sort out the whispers he'd heard and not understood at the time from the story as he'd pieced it together later. "He and your mother couldn't have been here for more than a couple of months. He fell from the staircase in his house. It was the sort of fall that nine times out of ten, you might walk away from with nothing more than bruises or a broken leg. He was just unlucky."

"That staircase." Her eyes went wide and dark. "Lydia showed me his portrait. She didn't say that was where he died."

"She probably didn't want to upset you." Now he'd done just that, but she'd wanted to know.

"I'd rather have the truth, no matter how upsetting." Her mouth set firmly.

"I believe you would."

She toyed with her spoon, turning it between her fingers. "My mother left shortly after that."

"Right after the funeral, I think." He seemed to hear an echo of his mother's voice. Left town right away, poor thing. Not that there was anything to keep her here. "Apparently no one knew she was pregnant."

"No." She said it softly, almost mournfully. "I was born six months later."

Maybe it was his turn to ask a question. "Why didn't your mother name your father? She'd have been entitled to support. Why keep it such a secret?"

"My great-aunt said that when I was born, Gracie was afraid Trey's family would try to take me away, but she gradually came to feel it was wrong not to tell his father. When I was six months old, she left me with my aunt, saying she was going to Savannah to talk to Trey's father about me. She never came back."

"Never came back?" He echoed the words, startled. "What do you mean?"

"She died." Her lips closed in a thin line, as if whatever else she knew, she wasn't sharing.

"When she was coming here, you mean?"

"An accident, my aunt always said. So my aunt brought me up. I suppose it was wrong of her to keep my father's identity a secret, but I can't be angry—she was trying to protect me."

He thought that over. "Protect?"

She nodded, eyes clouded. "That was what she said, when she was dying. I'm not sure what she was thinking. I guess she blamed Trey and his family for my mother's unhappiness. For the fact that she never came home again."

She never came home again. It was as mournful as the refrain from a haunting ballad.

"I'm sorry." The words were inadequate—he knew that. Whether Corrie was really Trey's daughter or not, she'd had a rough time of it. "I wish I could share a lot of happy memories of growing up with Trey, but I'm the wrong gen-cration. You really need to talk with Eulalie. Or Lydia."

"I know." She seemed to make an effort to shake off the shadows of the past. "Actually, I intended to talk with Eu-lalie today, but Deidre said she was out. That was how I ended up going to River Street with Deidre."

"Deidre—" He stopped, shrugged. "I was going to try and make up some excuse for her, but I can't think of one."

"Deidre's a grown woman. Her behavior isn't your re-sponsibility."

The instinct to deny that was so strong it startled him. Of course he was responsible for Deidre, just as he was respon-sible for the rest of them. Like it or not, they were family.

But if Corrie was Trey's daughter, then she was family, too, wasn't she?

Maybe it was safer to avoid that subject altogether. "Will you tell me something?"

She glanced up, expression wary. "What?"

"When I found you tonight—something had happened to scare you. What was it?"

She was still for the space of a breath. Then she seemed to make up her mind. "Someone was following me."

He studied her face. She looked a little defensive, as if she expected him to dismiss the idea as a figment of her imagination.

"Are you sure it wasn't just someone walking the same direction?"

"Someone who stopped when I stopped? Who slid back into the hedges when I turned around to look?" Her shoulders moved a little, as if to shake off the memory. "Just before you came, he was closing in on me. That's why I went into the street. You must have seen him."

He frowned. "I was looking for you. When I spotted you, you were out in the street. There was someone, behind you, on the sidewalk. I didn't notice anything except that it was a man."

He hadn't been paying attention—the man had been nothing but a dark silhouette. All his focus had been on Corrie. He'd been swamped with relief at finding her safe.

"It could have been any ordinary mugger, I suppose." Corrie sounded willing to accept that theory, but some emotion was held in reserve under the calm expression she showed him.

The same recklessness he'd felt earlier surged through him again. "What if it wasn't?"

Her eyes met his, and something at once angry and familiar leaped between them. "All right, what if it wasn't?

What if it wasn't an accident that I fell in front of that car, either? You tell me. Where do I go from there?"

He stared back at her, baffled, unable to look away. He didn't know. That was the problem—he didn't know.

Corrie framed the garden fountain in her viewfinder the next afternoon, trying to concentrate on the photograph and forget the worries that battered at her brain. At least, if nothing else, she'd have some pictures to remind her of her father's birthplace.

Unfortunately, the worries were not so easily dismissed. Lucas—what had he really thought of her story of being followed the previous night? For a while, sitting across from him in the candlelight, she'd almost thought he believed her. That he was on her side.

But that was foolishness. Lucas had no reason to side with her against the people he considered his family and every reason to want her gone. He'd hired a private detective to investigate her. Would he stop at hiring someone to frighten her enough that she'd leave?

A small shudder worked through her. Her mother had set out to see Trey's family, and her mother had died. She hadn't told Lucas that whole story, and she didn't intend to, but she couldn't let herself forget it. Now she was here, and someone seemed intent on scaring her away. Had they done the same to Gracie? At least she couldn't suspect Lucas of that. He'd just been a child then.

She frowned at the fountain. She couldn't pretend that spark of attraction between them didn't exist. But she also couldn't let herself trust him, or assume that he'd help her.

He'd seemed willing to talk about Trey the night before, but the few things he'd told her hadn't really amounted to much. It was all very well for Ann to tell her to talk to them, but Lucas and Jason were the only ones willing to talk, and they were the ones who knew the least.

Eulalie and Lydia had been remarkably evasive for the past two days—gone for most of the day, doing good works, apparently. Eulalie's volunteer schedule didn't seem to be as prestigious as Lydia's, but she took her pink lady service at the hospital as seriously as Lydia took sitting on the board of the art institute.

She glanced at her watch. Eulalie should be home by now. Maybe she'd be fortunate enough to catch her without the rest of the family around.

She walked quickly toward Eulalie's door, but as she approached, she saw that her hopes were doomed to disappointment. Lucas came in the gate from the street. He nodded, striding along the walk to join her.

"Going to Eulalie's?"

"She's been out most of the day, but I was hoping to talk to her."

"She'll be home by now." He opened the door without bothering to knock. "She picked Jason up from his summer arts program."

"Does he enjoy that?"

Lucas paused at the foot of the stairs, frowning as if the question merited a serious answer. "I think he does. He wanted to join a recreation program, but Eulalie thought it would be too much for him."

She knew better than to offer an opinion, but Lucas was looking at her as if he expected one, so she may as well. "Does his doctor agree with that?"

"Dr. Walker is an old friend of Eulalie's. I doubt that he would openly disagree with her."

"I see."

"Aren't you going to say anything else?"

She raised her brows. "You nearly bit my head off the last time I ventured an opinion."

"That was because I thought you were—" He stopped, apparently realizing where that statement was taking him.

"—just a waitress," she finished for him.

His lips tightened. "You know what I mean. I didn't realize you had any special expertise with children then."

She resisted the temptation to needle him on the subject of prejudging people, especially since she was guilty of that herself. "If you're asking, I've had asthmatic children in my physical education classes a number of times. They've usually benefited from physical activity. It's tough for a kid to feel that he can't do what his friends do."

"You think we're overprotecting Jason."

She wasn't sure what to make of the intensity in his voice. "I'm not a doctor. If you're not satisfied that Jason's doctor is impartial, you ought to take him to someone else. I'm sure Savannah has specialists in childhood asthma."

"I suppose so." His expression hadn't changed, but somehow she sensed a barricade, as if there were more to this conversation than a child's asthma. For a moment she thought he'd say something else, but he shook his head slightly and gestured for her to precede him up the stairs.

She could hardly expect him to confide in her. In his eyes she was a nuisance, if not an outright enemy.

They reached the top of the stairs and turned toward the parlor. They were almost at the doorway when Deidre's voice rang out. "I'm telling you I have proof that that woman is a fraud. What else do you want?"

Lucas's hand had tightened on her arm. She released herself. "I think that's my cue, don't you?"

She walked into the room. Deidre, face flushed, held something in her hand. Eulalie, looking distressed, sank down onto the sofa next to Lydia, who was frowning at Deidre as if she were a dubious piece of art. Ainsley, in the far corner, seemed to be trying to distance himself from the rest.

"Maybe you'd like to confront me with this proof of yours." She would not let her smile falter as they all swung to stare at her.

"Deidre, please…" Eulalie began, but her voice faded at a look from her daughter.

"Fine." Deidre thrust the paper in her hand toward Lucas. "She studied up on the family before she came, so she'd sound plausible, and Uncle Baxter is so senile he'd accept anything she told him. You didn't believe me when I told you she was a fraud, but there's the proof."

She didn't need a closer look to know it was the paper that had disappeared from her room.

"Deidre, this doesn't prove anything." Lucas sounded as if his patience had reached the breaking point. "First you go off and strand Corrie without a ride home, and then you come up with this nonsense."

"It's a list—"

"I know it's a list of the family. Baxter's attorneys gave Corrie the information. They thought she ought to know who she'd meet when she arrived."

Her anger was burning hot enough that she even resented Lucas for defending her. "They left out a few things." She plucked the paper from his hand. "They didn't mention that you were the kind of people who'd search my room and steal my belongings. Or try to have me run down in the street."

"Well." The voice from the doorway had everyone turning. Baxter Manning stood there, watching them, a thin smile on his lips. "It looks as if I've come home at just the right time, doesn't it?"

SEVEN

It had been one of the most uncomfortable meals Lucas could remember partaking of in Baxter's house, and that was saying something. After his surprise arrival, which had obviously not been a surprise to his staff, Baxter had insisted that the whole family join him for dinner, blandly ignoring the discomfort that caused in several quarters.

Baxter had sat back and watched with sardonic amusement as Deidre and Ainsley fought over nothing. He hadn't even intervened when Deidre had turned her sharp tongue on Corrie.

Lucas turned his head slightly. Corrie wasn't outwardly perturbed, but he sensed her tension across several feet of mahogany tabletop.

The polished table, the flickering candles, the vase of yellow roses in the center of the table—anyone looking at the scene would have thought it a festive family dinner. Only the people around the table knew how untrue that was.

Lydia put down her china cup with a tiny, musical chink. She slid her chair back, and the movement had an air of finality. "It's good to have you home again, Baxter. I'll say good-night now."

A small rustle went around the table, as if Lydia's retreat

gave them all permission to depart. Since Jason was leaning sleepily against him, it was time.

"I'll say good-night, as well." He started to get up, but Baxter stilled him with a small gesture.

"I'd appreciate your staying for a few minutes." His tone was polite, but it was nevertheless a command. "Perhaps Eulalie would see that Jason gets to bed."

"Of course." Eulalie got up, holding out her hand to Jason.

The others filtered out, saying polite good-nights, leaving only Baxter, Corrie and him in the candlelight.

Lucas expected Baxter's usual demand for a detailed accounting of all that had gone on at the company while he was away. Instead, he turned toward Corrie.

"Tell me. Have you finished what you came here to do?"

It might have been a polite inquiry from host to guest, if it hadn't been for the steel in Baxter's tone. Baxter disliked Corrie. He didn't know her, but he disliked her, probably because he considered her a fraud or an opportunist. Or possibly because she was a reminder of Trey.

"No. I haven't." Corrie pushed the china cup and saucer away from her with an air of rejection.

"Please don't tell me that my family hasn't cooperated. I'm sure I asked them to make you welcome."

The mockery in his tone was evident. A faint flush came up in Corrie's cheeks, but she met his gaze squarely. "I suspect they knew exactly how to interpret that."

One point to Corrie, but Lucas didn't like the way Baxter's mouth thinned.

"It's been a difficult situation for everyone." Common sense told him to stay out, but he couldn't help wanting to take the pressure off Corrie. "Especially since no one knows yet whether to welcome Corrie as a long-lost cousin or not."

Corrie's gaze clashed with his, and he suspected she'd be just as happy if he didn't try to help.

"I'm not looking for welcome or acceptance. I simply want an opportunity to know something of my father."

"If he is your father," Baxter snapped. "Even if he is—"

"You've already made it clear that I can expect nothing from you. Fine. I don't want anything, except for someone to talk to me honestly about Trey."

He saw the flare of anger in Baxter's face. It was there each time someone mentioned Trey, although Corrie couldn't know.

"I've given you the opportunity to do what you said you wanted. It's hardly my fault if you haven't succeeded."

It was definitely his fault, but he'd never admit it.

Corrie shot to her feet. "Are you telling me to leave?"

For a moment he thought Baxter would tell her to do just that. Lucas could see the exact moment when he decided to turn into a sick old man who was being badgered, instead.

"Who said anything about leaving? I don't want you to leave." His voice had a waver that Lucas wasn't sure whether to believe in or not.

"Then talk to me about Trey." She didn't back down an inch.

Baxter leaned his forehead on his hand, as if to shield his eyes from the light. "Not now. In a day or two."

Corrie looked as if she'd like to push but didn't quite dare. "I'll look forward to talking with you tomorrow, then." She nodded to Lucas and walked quickly out of the room.

Lucas waited until her footsteps had faded. Then he frowned at Baxter. "You can drop the infirm act. She's gone."

Baxter glared at him. "What makes you think it's an act? You're not my doctor."

"No, but I've known you all my life. And I'd like to know just what this situation with Corrie is all about."

"What do you mean? I'm trying to be fair to the girl."

"You're not being fair at all. You send her here, not giving us any indication of what you think about her. You can hardly expect this to be anything but uncomfortable for her."

Baxter waved that away. "She agreed to my terms. She knew what she was getting into."

"Did she?" He wished he could see into Baxter's motives. "It's still not fair to her. If she's Trey's daughter—"

"She's not." Baxter's gaze turned frosty.

"I hired an investigator. According to him, everything she's told us about herself is true."

Baxter's white eyebrows lifted. "That was very enterprising of you."

"I wanted to be sure you weren't taken for a ride." *You're my responsibility.* Baxter wouldn't admit that, but it was true.

"I'm not such a fool."

"But if she is Trey's child…"

"She's Grace's daughter. That doesn't mean Trey is her father."

He thought of what Corrie's response had been. Do the math. Unless they assumed Gracie had been having an affair during her few months in Savannah—but Baxter could do the math as well as he could.

"She could be Trey's child." He met Baxter's gaze. "You must have thought that, or why would you send her here?"

Baxter shoved his chair back with a sudden spurt of energy, rising to his feet. "That's not your business."

"Yes, it is." He was pushing harder than he usually did with Baxter, but this was important. "Corrie's presence affects everyone here. You must realize that."

The sudden spark in Baxter's eyes startled him. "Yes. It's stirred everyone up. It will do you all good."

Lucas could only stare at him as the truth slowly formed in his mind. "This isn't about Corrie at all, is it? You don't care whether she's your grandchild."

"Why else would I bring her here?"

"Because of us. All of us. You're using Corrie as a threat to warn everyone else to follow your wishes. That's it, isn't it?"

Baxter didn't answer. He smiled, turned and walked out of the room, leaving Lucas baffled, angry and disturbed.

In spite of his promises the night he'd arrived, Baxter still hadn't talked to her about Trey. Corrie walked down Bay Street two days later—slowly, because the heat and humidity demanded that.

She could hardly force the issue with a man who pleaded illness, but her frustration was growing. What was the point in her being here, if people wouldn't talk to her about her father?

At least she'd finally managed to corner Lydia. They'd lunched together, at a quaint tearoom patronized mainly by elderly women in hats. Lydia had smiled at the hats, but maintained the food was worth it.

She, at least, had been willing to talk, telling the kind of stories Corrie had come to Savannah to hear—stories of Trey as a child, getting into mischief and being forgiven for the price of a smile by an indulgent father. Corrie had formed an image of a boy who had been thoroughly spoiled by his doting father after his mother's death, but had managed to maintain a sweetness of disposition in spite of that.

Corrie stopped in front of an antique shop, staring in the window. That charm had been what attracted her mother, she supposed, along with the polished sophistication Gracie had probably never run into before.

She'd been thinking that she'd learned nothing since coming to Savannah, but that wasn't true. Unfortunately, what she'd learned only made her feel more isolated.

I'm not sure what I wanted, Lord. I feel as if I'll never really know who I am until I understand what happened to my parents. Maybe that's foolish and self-centered, but please, help me to understand.

She moved away from the display of pewterware and glanced down the street. There, ahead of her, a familiar figure turned into a doorway. Ainsley. Shouldn't he be at work? She glanced up at the clock on City Hall. Well, he might be on his lunch break. The office, she knew, was just a few blocks down Bay Street. But there had been something almost furtive about the way Ainsley had looked around that gave her pause.

She reached the doorway and stopped, looking for a sign. Nothing. The door, glass-fronted, gave no clue to what was inside. Through it, she could make out what appeared to be a row of folding chairs.

Impelled by curiosity and some vague sense of responsibility, she opened the door and slipped inside.

She found herself in a cavernous room, dark after the bright sunshine outside. She took a step forward and bumped into the back of a folding chair. She stood for a moment, letting her eyes become accustomed to the dimness, and realized she was in some sort of auditorium.

No, a theater. Down front, the stage was lit and empty, but while she watched, Ainsley came out from the wings, gesturing and saying something to a man behind him. His face was more animated than she'd ever seen it, startling her so much that her hand moved involuntarily on the chair, and the metal seats clattered together.

Both men looked up at the sound. Ainsley's face darkened. He jumped down from the stage and started toward her, the other man following.

She walked toward him, trying to smile as if running into him this way was an everyday event. The glare he fixed on her didn't encourage her to believe he bought that.

"What are you doing here?" He planted his hands on his hips, all his usual youthful diffidence gone. "Are you spying on me?"

She resisted the urge to take a step back. "Of course not. I saw you on the street and—"

"Couldn't resist the urge to see what I was up to." He glared. "Ready to run to Uncle Baxter with a report on me?"

"Why would he care what you do on your lunch hour?" Really, these people had an odd idea of what interested Baxter Manning.

Before he could answer, the other man elbowed him aside. "Ainsley, introduce me. Is this the new cousin you've been telling me about?" He held out his hand, giving her that charming smile Southern men seemed to have patented. "I'm Ainsley's friend, Patrick Tarleton."

"It's nice to meet you. I'm Corrie Grant."

Patrick was taller than Ainsley, with dark hair and eyes and a dimple that showed when he smiled. "You have to forgive Ainsley. He gets a tad obsessed about his great-uncle's attitude."

Ainsley managed a rather sick-looking smile. "Right. I…I'm sorry. I guess I overreacted."

"That's okay." She could forget if he could. After all, she had followed him into the building. She glanced around, relieved to get the subject off Baxter. "Is this a theater?"

Patrick chuckled. "Well, it will be if we ever get our first production underway. We're working on a frayed shoe-string right now."

So this was Ainsley's secret. It hardly seemed worth the fuss of keeping it from anyone. "Are you an actor, Ainsley?"

"Never." He pushed the idea away with both hands. "Pat's the actor. I'm designing the sets."

That explained the sketchbook he'd been unwilling to let her see. "That's great. I'd think your family would be proud."

"No, they…they wouldn't understand. Honestly. You don't know them. Uncle Baxter would say I'm wasting my time."

"Can't you do what you want on your own time?" She'd like to see someone try to tell her what she should do for a hobby, but Ainsley was obviously terrified of his great-uncle's opinions.

"You can't tell them." Panic flickered in his eyes. "Promise me you won't say anything to anyone, even Lucas."

"Of course she'll promise." Patrick's hand closed over hers, and it almost sounded as if he were warning her.

She shook off the idea. "If it's that important to you, of course. Just let me know when your opening is, so I can come and see it."

"We will." Patrick, still holding her arm, was urging her toward the door. No doubt about it—she was being given the bum's rush, in the politest possible way, of course.

"I'll see you at the house, Ainsley." She barely had time to get the words out before Patrick had the door open and was escorting her through.

"I'm sorry." He paused in the doorway, lowering his

voice. "Ainsley didn't mean anything. He really is irrational about his great-uncle. I know we can count on you."

She had to blink at the persuasiveness of his smile. "I wouldn't give him away." Because of Ainsley, not because of you, she thought but didn't say. "Goodbye. Let me know when the opening night is."

The door closed behind her, and she stood for a moment, wondering if Ainsley really were being irrational about Baxter. Did the man exert such control over every aspect of his dependents' lives? Maybe that told her more than anything else had about Trey.

She walked on, turning the realization over in her mind. Ainsley reacted by hiding what he was doing. Trey, apparently, had reacted with rebellion. Maybe she had to stop thinking about him as her father and think about him as a young man, not even as old as Ainsley was now. He hadn't been much more than a college kid, still trying to figure out who he was.

She was only a half block down the street when she recognized the tall figure coming toward her. Was the whole family out and about on Bay Street today?

"Corrie." Lucas stopped, looking a little startled. "What brings you downtown today?"

"I had a lunch date with Lydia." The longing to say something to him about Ainsley, to have him laugh at Ainsley's fear, was strong. But she couldn't speak. She'd promised.

"I hope Lydia was forthcoming."

She nodded. "She talked about Trey when he was a child. I appreciated it, especially since Baxter still hasn't kept his promise."

He grimaced. "I'm afraid Baxter remembers what he wants to. Keep after him, though."

"I will."

They stood for a moment. She ought to move away, let Lucas get on with whatever he was doing, but she was oddly resistant to walking away. Lucas, in spite of his doubts about her, was at least honest with her.

"I wanted to tell you that I took your advice," he said.

She looked at him blankly. "What advice?"

"I took Jason to see a specialist in childhood asthma."

"You did? I'm glad." She wanted to ask what the doctor said, but it wasn't her place.

"He started Jason on some new medication. And gave me a lecture."

"A lecture?"

"On overprotecting him. In his opinion, if his asthma is under control, which it is, Jason should be able to do what other kids do."

She didn't want to say I told you so, but her smile probably said it all.

Lucas's eyes crinkled. "Yes, I know. You told me. But now you have to pay the price for your interference."

"And what would that be?"

"Tomorrow afternoon you, Jason and I are going horseback riding. Okay?"

She actually felt herself choke up. "You mean it? Lucas, he'll be so happy. Of course I'll go."

"Good." His fingers closed over hers, and their warmth seemed to travel right up her arm. "You'd better be as good a cowgirl as you claim to be, or I'll be seriously disappointed in you."

"You won't be," she said, her heart ridiculously light. "I promise."

* * *

Corrie leaned forward in the car, just as eager for her first sight of the farm as Jason was. A lane stretched between two white gateposts, bordered by a dense growth of deep green pines, their trunks as straight as sentinels.

"We're here," Jason crowed. "I love to come to Daddy's farm."

She shot a questioning look at Lucas. "This is your place?" Somehow she'd pictured a stable where they'd rent horses.

"It belonged to my grandparents. And their grandparents before that, I guess. The Santees started out as farmers." He smiled, his face relaxing as if just being here eased his mind. "It's in the blood, no matter what I do."

"But you don't run it yourself." Every time she thought she had Lucas pegged, he showed her an unexpected side.

He shook his head. "The land is rented out to a neighboring farmer, for the most part. I have a caretaker who keeps up the house and barn and takes care of the horses."

He drove past a white frame two-story farmhouse, its flower beds a riot of color, and on back down the lane to a red barn, settled under the shade of the pines and live oaks as if it had been there always.

"I spent a lot of time here as a boy." Lucas got out, and she thought there was regret in the look he turned on Jason as his son slid from the car and ran toward the barn.

"But not Jason?" They followed the boy more slowly.

"No." His face tightened, and for a moment she thought he wouldn't say anything else. "Julia didn't care for it, and she always objected when I wanted to bring him."

"Did coming here ever trigger an attack?"

"No. But it didn't seem worth arguing about every time."

She thought she could read the rest of the story in his face. Julia had been overprotective, and when Jason developed asthma, it seemed her fears were justified.

"It's a shame," she said, keeping her voice carefully neutral, "that he hasn't had the childhood experiences you enjoyed."

Lucas frowned. "I have to keep him safe," he said, almost to himself.

She hadn't found an answer to that when they stepped into the barn, and then every other thought was driven from her mind by a wave of homesickness. Everything— the fresh scent of hay, the rustle of straw, the stamping and soft whickers as the horses moved at their entrance—it all reminded her of home so strongly that her throat choked.

Jason already clung to a stall door, patting the muzzle that the stall's occupant thrust toward him. "I want to ride Queenie, Daddy. Can I?"

"You have to ask Mr. Davis." Lucas nodded toward the elderly black man who came toward them.

"Can I, Mr. Davis? Please?"

The caretaker pushed his ball cap to the back of his head, seeming to consider the request, but Corrie read the answer in the twinkle in his eyes.

"Well, I reckon, if your daddy says it's okay."

"Queenie's my favorite." Jason's smile was blissful. "What about Cousin Corrie? Who does she get to ride?"

"Jason, slow down." Lucas's face warmed as he shook hands with the elderly man. "Corrie, this is Ephraim Davis. He looks after everything here."

Corrie felt as if she were being measured as they shook hands and exchanged pleasantries.

Finally he gave a satisfied nod. "I guess Ms. Corrie should ride Belle. Seems like she knows her way around horses."

She hoped that didn't mean he intended to test her riding skills, but when she saw the dainty little mare, she fell instantly in love.

"She's Arabian, isn't she?" She ran her hand along the mare's characteristic dish-shaped face.

"Half-Arabian," Lucas said, opening the stall door. "Go ahead, bring her out."

She was conscious of his gaze as she led the mare out of the stall, hooking her to the cross-ties he indicated. He stood for a moment, watching as she picked up the curry brush to run over the mare's back before putting on the saddle blanket, and nodded.

"Ephraim said I'd better hang around to help you, but you obviously know what you're doing."

She hefted the saddle, swinging it easily into place and bending to reach for the cinch. "Did you think I was lying about knowing horses?" She ought to be used to his automatic skepticism by now, but it still caught her off guard.

"Not lying." He led a black gelding from the next stall. Sturdy and strong-muscled, he must stand at least sixteen hands high. "Maybe exaggerating."

She whistled. "Well, you weren't exaggerating about the quality of your horseflesh. That's a nice animal."

"Wish I could spend more time with him." A shadow of regret crossed his face. "I used to think it a crime to own a fine horse and not ride it."

Odd, that Lucas seemed to feel he couldn't do something he wanted to. Or maybe shouldn't do it. "Well, if the doctor feels it's okay for Jason to ride, that will be a nice thing for the two of you to do together."

"Yes." He didn't look relieved, and she wondered how big a battle he'd had with Eulalie over bringing his son here today.

"Lucas—" She stopped. It wasn't her business, and she had to stop speaking her mind around these people.

"What?"

The other two had started out of the barn, toward the paddock, but Lucas stood close to her. The horses nuzzled each other behind them, moving restlessly.

She smiled, shaking her head. "It's not my business."

"I think I can guess, but it's not as easy as you might suppose." He stared toward the boy and the old man, silhouetted in the barn doorway. "I can't make a mistake with Jason."

"Every parent makes mistakes." Why was he so hard on himself?

He shook his head, but he clasped her hand for a moment, setting up the by-now-familiar reaction. "Thanks, Corrie. For caring."

He let go, starting toward the others. She still seemed to feel the imprint of his fingers on hers, and she tried to shake the feeling away. What was she thinking? She couldn't let herself feel anything for Lucas.

EIGHT

It soon became evident that Mr. Davis didn't intend to let anyone out of his sight until he was satisfied with their ability. Fortunately, Jason proved to be a natural. The look of pride on his face when he finally was allowed to trot around the paddock in his father's wake was something to behold.

After an hour, the elderly man swung the gate open. "Mind you stay on the mowed trail or the dirt road," he cautioned. "I heard someone shooting off toward Patterson's Creek yesterday. Some folks don't care whether it's hunting season or not."

"We won't go far." Lucas had to do no more than shift his weight, and the big gelding moved through the gate. "Jason, you keep Queenie behind the other horses, and she'll follow right along."

She half expected Jason to protest, but he nodded, obviously too thrilled to be here to want more.

"And don't let her put her head down to eat," Davis cautioned. "She'll try it as soon as you get near any fresh grass."

"Okay." Jason dug his heels into the mare's side, and Queenie ambled through the gate after the other horses.

"We'll stay on the road at first," Lucas said, pulling over to let Corrie move up beside him. "How do you like Belle?"

"She's a darling." She patted the sleek neck, feeling the mare dance eagerly beneath her. "She'd love a nice long canter about now."

"Not today." Lucas glanced back over his shoulder at Jason.

"I understand." It wouldn't be fair to make Jason watch something he wasn't ready to try. "Thank you for this, Lucas. For my sake, as well as Jason's."

He smiled. "It's easy to please you, if this is all it takes."

"It feels like home." Again she felt that tightening in her throat.

"You're not going to tell me you ride beneath live oaks in Wyoming, are you?"

A trailing bit of Spanish moss detached itself from an overhead branch and touched her shoulder. "The vegetation's entirely different. But the feeling's the same." She stretched, enjoying the rhythmic movement of her body in tune with the horse's sway. "I must be getting used to it here, though. It doesn't even seem claustrophobic to me anymore." The lane wound ahead of them, so thickly lined with trees and shrubs that it seemed it would disappear entirely.

"That's good. We wouldn't want you to panic. So you rode a lot when you were a kid."

He seemed genuinely interested, so she talked a little about growing up out West, turning her head so that Jason could hear. He was soon peppering her with questions, eager to know about a life that must seem very exotic in comparison to his.

They reached a small stream and stopped to let the horses drink.

Corrie dismounted, stretching. "It's been way too long since I've been in the saddle."

"Sore tomorrow?" Lucas gave her a friendly rub between the shoulder blades, as impersonal as if he patted the horse. It wasn't his fault that she felt that touch right to the marrow of her bones.

"Probably a little. I'd better start jogging while I'm here. I'm sure not getting any other exercise."

"You're welcome to come out and ride any time you want. I'll give you Ephraim's number—just call and let him know."

"Thank you." The offer surprised and pleased her. Maybe— "Tell me something," she said abruptly, before she could talk herself out of it.

His eyebrows lifted. "If I can."

"Do you believe me now?" It shouldn't matter so much what he thought, but it did.

He didn't give her that shuttered expression. Instead, he regarded her gravely for a long moment. "I believe you're who you say you are. I believe you're Gracie's daughter, and that you honestly think you're Trey's child."

She shouldn't feel disappointed. He didn't owe her anything more. "Thank you."

His smile flickered. "I'm not sure being related to Baxter Manning is an asset, you know."

"You may have a point there." She returned the smile, turning to mount up again. At least she and Lucas weren't enemies any longer. That was enough to lighten her heart.

Lucas let the horses move into a jog trot on the way back to the barn, watching his son attentively. Jason bounced along, face flushed with such pure delight that pleasure flooded Corrie.

It had been a good day in so many ways. Maybe the best day she'd had since she came to Savannah.

"Do you ordinarily ride a lot when you're at home?" Lucas picked up their conversation as if no time had intervened.

"It depends. While my aunt was sick, I didn't have time for it. Otherwise, I have a friend who's a rancher, and I usually go riding with him once a week or so."

"A friend. As in boyfriend?"

She smiled. "Mike was seventy-two his last birthday. He'd be tickled pink to be thought of as my boyfriend."

"No special someone in your life now?"

"No." Her love life wasn't Lucas's business, but if they were able to talk at a personal level, that meant they were moving into being friends. "I date. I'm not a hermit. But somehow…" She hesitated, the thought still clarifying in her mind. "Maybe I've always felt as if I had unfinished business to take care of before I let myself get serious about anyone. I need to know who I am."

"You're Corrie Grant. Isn't that enough?"

"I guess it should be." She tried to be honest. "It should be enough to know that I'm God's child, but the questions are still there. I'm not even sure what it is I need to know. I just know there's a hole that needs filling."

There. She'd told him more about her feelings than she'd told anyone, except possibly Ann. If he didn't understand—well, at least she'd been honest.

They'd reached the barn, and Lucas dismounted and stood looking at her as she slid down from the saddle. "I hope you find it, Corrie. Whatever it is you're looking for."

"Thank you." The words sounded choked, and she had to clear her throat.

Mr. Davis was already helping Jason with his horse, so she took the saddle off Belle, slinging it over the stall bar. Lucas handed her a brush and took one for himself.

They worked in companionable silence for a few minutes. She could hear the soft sounds the horses made as they were groomed, as if expressing approval of the process. A fly buzzed lazily against a windowpane, and Belle stamped her foot and swished her tail. It was all familiar and satisfying.

She glanced over at Lucas. "What about you?" she asked softly. "Is there someone serious in your life?"

"No." His face tightened, shutting her out.

The brush in her hand stilled, and Belle moved restlessly. She began stroking again. He couldn't have intended that to be as curt as it sounded.

"Not even someone to go out with now and then? You know what they say about all work and no play."

She meant it lightly. She wasn't prepared for the shuttered face he turned on her.

"That's not your concern."

For a moment she just stared at him, and then her anger flared. "In other words, you can ask me anything you want, no matter how personal it is, but I can't reciprocate."

He tossed his brush in the box, face tight. "Leave it alone, Corrie."

"Why should I? Do you know how obnoxiously superior that is?" Being angry with him was a lot better than being hurt by his attitude.

"I don't owe you—"

Ephraim's urgent voice stopped him. "Lucas, the boy— something's wrong."

Jason leaned against the stall, bracing himself on one hand. His face was white, eyes wide, his breath rasping.

Corrie's heart thudded, anger vanishing in a rush of concern. He was having an asthma attack, poor child.

Lucas reached him first, pulling an inhaler out of his pocket. "Easy, son. You're going to be fine. We'll get you to the doctor right away."

He lifted Jason in his arms, elbowing his way past Corrie as if she weren't even there. He was nearly to the car before she caught up with him.

"Let me hold Jason." She grabbed his arm. "You have to drive—I don't know the way."

For an instant she thought he'd refuse. Then he gave a curt nod and transferred Jason to her arms. He had a tender smile for his son.

But the look he turned on Corrie was enough to freeze her heart. He looked as if he hated her.

Lucas stood in the hallway for a moment, listening for any sounds from the upstairs bedroom. Jason had seemed fine after his breathing treatment, but Lucas couldn't relax until his son had gotten through the night without incident.

Eulalie had finally gone back to her house once Jason was settled in bed. She'd been too polite to say I told you so, but the words had been there in every reproachful glance.

A vise tightened around his heart. She didn't have to remind him of how wrong he'd been in the past. He lived with that every day.

The doorbell rang, interrupting what would have been a fruitless excursion into memory. He couldn't change the past. He could only control what he did now.

He crossed the hallway to the front door, hoping that his mother-in-law hadn't decided to return.

"Corrie." He should have known she'd come.

She lingered on the doorstep, looking unsure of her reception. "I don't want to disturb you. I just came to see how Jason is."

He swung the door wider. "Come in, please. He's asleep finally, and he's doing much better."

She'd changed from the jeans she'd worn earlier to a dress of some soft material—probably in deference to having dinner with Baxter. She hesitated a moment longer and then stepped inside, shooting him a fleeting glance.

"I wasn't sure I'd be welcome."

"Of course you're welcome in my house. Anytime."

Although if he had any sense, he wouldn't say that. Corrie attracted him in a way no woman had in a long time, if ever, but anything between them was completely impossible.

She tilted her head, and the overhead light struck gold in her hair. "You were angry with me for encouraging Jason about the horses."

That would be an easy out, but he couldn't take it. "You weren't responsible. I am."

"I doubt that Eulalie sees it that way."

Probably not, but that was the least of his concerns. "Don't fret over Eulalie. She's not happy unless she has something to worry about." He nodded toward the family room. "Come and sit down."

She stepped through the archway, glancing around at the slightly shabby leather couches and the built-in bookshelves stuffed to the brim with everything from architecture texts to the picture books Jason had as a toddler. Somehow he couldn't bring himself to get rid of a once-loved book.

"This is nice. Very different from Baxter's house." She stopped, coloring slightly. "I didn't mean that—"

He smiled, feeling the tension that had ridden him for hours slip away. "I know exactly what you mean. Baxter's place is a beautiful museum."

"Yes."

Was she comparing that house to the one where she'd grown up? She probably couldn't help doing that. Baxter lived in what must seem like luxury to her, while his granddaughter, if she was that, lived in near-poverty.

Corrie crossed to the coffee table, where Jason's latest jigsaw puzzle was laid out. "This must be Jason's, since it's a paddock full of horses."

"He loves puzzles. Almost as much as horses." He motioned her to the couch and sat down next to her. "You can help me with it. He wanted this part of the barn finished, but his grandmother said it was bedtime, so I promised I'd do it for him."

Corrie bent over the puzzle, blond curls tumbling around her face. "My aunt was a puzzle fan, too. Not horses, though. Scenes of foreign countries we'd never be able to visit. She had a three-dimensional one of the Eiffel Tower that nearly drove us crazy." She fit a piece into the barn door. "About Jason and the horses—"

"There's no sense talking about it. We gave it a try, and it didn't work out." He grimaced. "As Eulalie pointed out numerous times."

"Eulalie loves him, I know. But she's not his parent."

He realized his hand was clenching and deliberately released it. "Let's not go over that again. I shouldn't have exposed Jason to something that likely to trigger an attack. I won't again."

"But you said he was all right." She surveyed him gravely. Why wouldn't the woman leave well enough alone? It was just as well he couldn't be interested in her, because she'd send him around the bend in a week and a half.

"He's all right now, but the attack shouldn't have happened. It was my fault."

"Why?" Her face was very close. "Why do you insist that it's your fault? Asthma is the most common chronic disease for children."

"I'm not responsible for those other children." He tossed down the puzzle piece that didn't seem to fit anywhere. "Just my son. I have to take care of him."

"You can't wrap him in a bubble. Kids with asthma should be able to be just as active—"

"I won't take chances with him!" Why wouldn't she understand? "I didn't take Julia's health problems seriously, and she died. Isn't that enough to have on my conscience?"

He wanted the words back as soon as they were spoken, but it was too late. He could only stare at her, waiting for the look of revulsion to dawn in her eyes.

It didn't come. She just studied him, face serious. "Your wife died of ovarian cancer. Why would you think you're responsible?"

"I don't want to talk about it." He tried pulling the barricade back into place between them.

She reached out as if she intended to touch him and then seemed to think the better of it. "Tell me about her. About Julia."

He shook his head, but already the compulsion to make her understand was too great. "There's not much to say. Julia was beautiful. Fragile. And she died too young."

"Why fragile?" She looked as if she thought it an odd word choice, but she'd never known Julia.

"Because she was that. Always. She was like a piece of

delicate china." That fragility had attracted him at first. He'd seen himself as her protector. It was only later that he'd become impatient with it.

"Did she have some chronic illness?"

The matter-of-fact tone surprised him. "No. She just…" How could he explain Julia? "Eulalie always said Julia lived on her nerves. Anything stressful exhausted her."

Corrie didn't have to say what she thought of that. It was written all over her face.

"You don't understand." He could hear the defensiveness in his voice.

"No, I don't. I never had the luxury of indulging in nerves."

His jaw tightened painfully. "I thought that, too. That her complaints were imaginary—excuses to get out of things that she didn't want to do. I was impatient with her."

"Maybe you were right."

"I was wrong." He shot to his feet, unable to see the look of sympathy in her eyes. "I didn't take her complaints seriously. Not until we learned she had cancer."

He heard Corrie rise, felt her move closer to him. "Lucas, it wasn't your fault. You didn't cause her cancer."

"That's not the point."

Her hand closed on his arm, warm and firm. "It is the point. It's a terrible thing that she died, and it's natural for you to grieve. But feeling guilty is irrational. The fact that you were impatient with her imaginary ills doesn't make you guilty when she really became ill."

If he let himself listen to her, he might begin to believe her, but he couldn't do that. "I was responsible for her." He swung toward her, grasping her arms. "Don't you see that? I should have—"

"What, Lucas? What else could you have done?"

Her face was very close, and the caring in her eyes was so strong it startled him. And frightened him, because it made him want to pull her into his arms, to lose himself in the warmth of her embrace.

His hands tightened on her arms, and he saw the moment when the same longing flared in her eyes. She swayed toward him, in another instant they'd be kissing—

He let go of her abruptly, taking a quick step back. The light faded from her face, overtaken by confusion and embarrassment.

"I'm sorry." She spun and walked quickly out of the room. A moment later he heard the front door slam shut.

"I said, I think you should tell Corrie what she wants to know and send her home." Lucas pushed down his repugnance at what he felt forced to do. After what had nearly happened with Corrie the previous night, he couldn't pretend any longer that it was safe to have her around.

He glared at Baxter, who lounged in the massive leather chair behind the equally massive mahogany desk in his study. This situation was Baxter's fault, with his endless need to manipulate those around him.

"Why?" Baxter raised silvery brows.

She stirred up feelings that were better left buried—and not just about the family. He'd tried to dismiss Corrie's words about his guilt over Julia, but they kept coming back, over and over. Still, he certainly wouldn't say that to Baxter.

"Because what you're doing isn't fair to anyone."

Baxter waved that off with an imperious hand. "I'm a better judge of that than you are. Why aren't you at work?"

"This is more important." He leaned on the desk, wishing his feelings of old affection and concern didn't get in the way when he tried to deal with Baxter. "Talk to Corrie. She deserves that at least. Make provision for her. But get her out of here."

The old man's lips tightened at that. "I don't owe her anything. When did you go over to her side?"

"I haven't." He repressed the memory of Corrie's face, inches from his. "Still, everything I've learned tells me she's not a con artist. She believes she's Trey's daughter. And unless you can prove she's not—"

"I can't." Baxter clipped off the words. He slapped his palm down on a manila envelope that lay on his desk blotter. "Do you know what this is?"

Even upside down, he could read the return address of the testing laboratory. "The results of the DNA test? What did they say?"

Baxter's color deepened. "A lot of gibberish—safeguards, hedges, talk about how difficult it is."

He frowned. "I thought DNA testing was fairly straightforward. They use it to prove relationships to people who've been dead for hundreds of years, don't they?"

"If Edith were alive, apparently the results would be clearer." Baxter sounded as if his long-dead wife were to blame. "It seems there's some genetic marker in the female line that makes it more of a sure thing."

"So how sure is it?"

"She is probably Trey's child." He spat out the words.

"Probably doesn't get us very far. If you still think she's not—"

"I think she is." Baxter pushed himself to his feet with a shadow of his former energy. "It would be just like Trey to disappoint me this way."

"Disappoint you." He could only stare at Baxter. What

kind of man reacted like this to the knowledge that he had a grandchild?

"That's right. Disappoint me." The old man's voice rose, and his color darkened alarmingly. "I gave him everything, and he repaid me with constant rebellion and disappointment. He could have married into one of the best families in Georgia, and instead he picked an illiterate nobody—"

"Hardly illiterate." He tried to keep his voice calm, but he couldn't let that pass without comment. "Gracie may not have been well educated, but she graduated from high school with honors, according to the private investigator. And Corrie has a college degree."

"She isn't one of us." Baxter leaned heavily on his hands. "You see that. She'll never be one of us."

"No. She won't." She won't be tied hand and foot by tradition. She's strong, tough and independent. But saying those things would only madden Baxter further, and he had no desire to do that. "But she's your granddaughter. You'll have to tell her—she has a right to know the results of the DNA testing."

"Don't tell me what I have to do!" He fairly shouted the words. "I didn't owe her mother a thing, and I don't owe her, either. If Trey had lived, they'd have hung around his neck all his life, but he didn't even have the courtesy to clean up his own messes."

The anger Lucas had been holding back finally broke through his iron control. "Corrie may not be the grandchild you'd hoped for, but she's a decent person. Face the truth, Baxter. Ranting and raving didn't work with Trey, and they won't resolve things now."

"Don't speak to me that way." The words began forcefully, but faded to breathlessness. "I don't…I can't…" He sagged, leaning heavily against the desk. His color, which had been almost purple a moment earlier, faded to a sickly gray.

Lucas rounded the desk, heart pounding, reaching for him. "This isn't good for you. Sit down. I'll get you some water."

Baxter stared at him, eyes losing focus. Then he slumped forward, collapsing into Lucas's arms.

NINE

The sound of raised voices was so foreign to Baxter's household that Corrie stopped in her bedroom doorway, unsure what to do. Baxter's voice, then Lucas's—both sounding angry, both coming from the study that adjoined Baxter's bedroom.

She couldn't stand and eavesdrop, no matter how loud they were. She crossed quickly to the head of the stairs. She touched the railing just as she heard Lucas shout.

"Corrie! Mrs. Andrews!"

He wouldn't sound like that unless something was very wrong. Heart pounding, she spun and raced toward the study. She bolted through the door and came to a dead stop.

Baxter slumped over the desk, head nearly resting on the blotter. His face, what she could see of it, was ashen, his eyes unfocused. Lucas fumbled, trying to loosen the necktie Baxter wore even in the privacy of his own home.

She hurried toward them, first aid measures running through her mind. Luckily her CPR certification was up to date.

"Call an ambulance." She pushed Lucas's hands away and ripped the necktie free, jerking open the top few buttons to feel for a pulse on his neck. "Has he had a heart attack before?"

One of the many things she hadn't been privileged to know about her own grandfather. The pulse was there, weak, but there.

"Yes." Lucas already snatched up the phone, dialing 911. "He hates to admit there's anything wrong with him."

She bent over, checking his breathing. "Baxter." She raised her voice. "Look at me. Do you have medication to take? Aspirin?"

His eyes focused, and he tried to pull away from her. "Not an ambulance." His voice was stronger than she expected. "Call my doctor. Young Haverford."

She exchanged glances with Lucas, and he shrugged. She could imagine what he was thinking. That if Baxter weren't having a heart attack, disobeying his orders would probably bring one on.

"All right." Lucas broke the connection and began to punch in another number. "Tell Corrie where your medicine is."

She was already patting at his pockets, earning her a fierce glare.

"Medicine cabinet. Bottom shelf." He jerked away from her. His color was still bad, but he seemed stronger.

Lucas nodded, so she hurried through the door that connected the study to the master bedroom. Rich red brocade wallpaper, a gigantic four-poster bed, an Oriental carpet on the floor—her mind registered the details even as she raced across the room and into the adjoining master bath.

The medicine cabinet door stood ajar, and she pulled it the rest of the way, scanning the bottom shelf. Vitamins, arthritis medication—there it was, a vial of nitroglycerin.

She snatched it up and ran back to the study, taking the cap off as she went.

Baxter held out his hand, and she dropped the white tablet into it, watching to be sure he managed to get it into his mouth. He leaned back in the chair, head tilted, his eyes half-closed.

She glanced at Lucas, to see the same concern in his face that must be written on hers. Funny. Baxter had given her no possible reason to like him, but that didn't matter. She cared for him anyway.

Please, Lord. I don't suppose he'd want to know that I'm praying for him, but that doesn't matter. Be with him. Strengthen him.

She took a breath, knowing that there was something else that had to be said. *Forgive my resentment of him, Father. Help me to respect him as my grandfather, even if he never accepts me.*

The doctor arrived in less time than she'd have thought possible. Maybe this was one of those instances where money talked. He was followed by the housekeeper, voluble in her distress at not having heard Lucas call her. Between them, they managed to help Baxter to his bed. Then Corrie and Lucas were dismissed, politely but firmly, by Dr. Haverford.

"Mrs. Andrews will assist me." He opened a black bag that Corrie thought had gone out with the horse and buggy. "Please wait in the study."

Back in the study, with the door to the bedroom closed, she raised her eyebrows at Lucas. "*Young* Dr. Haverford? Somehow his white hair doesn't fit that description."

Lucas managed a smile. "I know. But his father was Baxter's doctor first, so Stan is stuck with being 'young' Haverford, even though he's semiretired."

"That's how he got here so fast."

"He lives just around the corner. A good thing, since Baxter demands his services fairly frequently."

Lucas crossed to the window, as if he couldn't stand still any longer. In spite of his calm tone, she read tension in the stiffness of his shoulders.

"Tell me something."

He turned to look at her. "What?"

"What were you and Baxter quarreling about?"

For a second she thought he wouldn't answer her at all. Then he shrugged. "You know Baxter. It's not difficult to quarrel with him."

That evasion probably meant they'd been quarreling about her. Why? Somehow she didn't think she'd get an answer to that question.

Her throat tightened. Last night she and Lucas had seemed closer than she'd have believed possible, right up until the moment when they'd nearly kissed. She'd probably never forget the expression on Lucas's face when he'd pulled away from her. That rejection was burned into her heart.

The bedroom door opened, putting an end to her fruitless line of thought. Dr. Haverford came out, closing the door softly behind him. He gaze touched on Corrie inquiringly, as if questioning her right to be there.

Lucas came toward him. "What's the verdict?"

Haverford turned to him with something like relief in his face. "Surprising as it seems, he's escaped again. He should be in the hospital, of course, but you know his attitude toward that."

"He'll die in his own bed," Lucas said, his tone dry. He'd obviously heard the words before. "What about caring for him here?"

"I'll set up round-the-clock nurses for a few days. Like it or not, he's going to stay in bed until I tell him otherwise." He smiled faintly. "I threatened to restrain him if he didn't behave."

"I wish I thought that would work." Lucas glanced toward the closed door, as if he expected to see Baxter come through it.

"I'll make certain the nurses are dragons who won't be intimidated by him." Haverford shook hands with Lucas, gave Corrie a doubtful nod and went out.

The room was very still after his footsteps had faded down the stairs. Lucas stood by the desk, frowning down at its surface. He touched a manila envelope lightly with his fingertips, then sent the frowning glance toward her.

"There's something you should know." His abrupt tone didn't encourage her to believe it was anything good.

"What?" She straightened, ready for whatever he intended to throw at her.

"Baxter received the results of those DNA tests."

She swallowed hard. Maybe she wasn't as ready as she'd hoped. "And?" She couldn't read anything in his face.

"Apparently they can't be positive, but the indications are that you're Trey's daughter."

Funny. It wasn't as much of a shock to her as Lucas might think. She'd never really doubted her mother. Still…

She tried to imagine what this might mean to her. Would it change anything at all?

Lucas was studiously avoiding her gaze. It took a while, but she finally got it.

"That's why he had the attack, isn't it?" The realization left an acrid taste in her mouth. "Knowing I'm Trey's child made him so angry it brought on the attack."

Lucas so clearly didn't want to tell her. Of course not. Underneath all his other qualities, Lucas was kind. But he was also truthful.

"Yes. I'm sorry."

Corrie touched the photo of her parents, her fingertips lingering on the young faces. She'd done her best, hadn't she? At least she'd proved to her own satisfaction that her mother had been an honest woman. That she was the daughter of Trey and Gracie's marriage.

That should be enough, Lord. Why do I still feel so empty?

The faded photograph didn't have any answers for her. Her parents' faces looked so incredibly young—younger and more naive than she was. What did she expect to learn about them that could mean any difference to her now?

She'd put the picture into her Bible at Psalm 139 for a reason. She smoothed the page, reading the words that she could say by heart.

> You know me inside and out, you know every bone in my body; You know exactly how I was made, bit by bit, how I was sculpted from nothing into something.

God knew her, as God knew all things. God understood what had brought Trey and Gracie together and what had split them apart. Maybe she never would.

She closed the Bible and laid it gently into her open suitcase. Her grandfather accepted now that she was his grandchild and knowing that had been enough to anger him into a heart attack. That was certainly a dramatic enough way of telling her that she had no place here.

Baxter's illness would succeed where other efforts had failed. The person, whoever it was, who'd pushed her in the street and followed her from the shop would be happy.

Deidre? She couldn't have done those things personally, but that didn't mean she couldn't have arranged them. She'd never know for sure now.

Corrie straightened, rubbing the back of her neck where the tension had gathered. Deciding she'd go home was a simple matter. Actually doing it, however, was more complicated. She'd have to make flight arrangements, tell the others she was leaving…

Her lips curved at that. They'd be happy with her for the first time since she'd walked into their lives. How odd that only the proof she was Trey's child had convinced her, finally, to leave.

Lucas was in the study, she knew. He'd been stationed there since the previous day, running the various businesses, reporting to Baxter as often as the nurses allowed. And the house was something of an armed camp, with Mrs. Andrews sniffing at the nurses, convinced that she could take better care of Baxter than they could.

She may as well start with Lucas, because he'd be the most difficult. She'd tell him of her decision. As for her grandfather—well, he might or might not want to say goodbye to her.

Before she could reconsider, she marched out of the bedroom and down the hall toward the study. The paneled door stood ajar, and she pushed it the rest of the way.

Lucas sat at the old-fashioned desk that dominated the room. A shaft of sunlight, coming through the side window, lit his hair with streaks of gold. Golden boy—that's what she'd thought the first time she saw him.

Now she knew better. In spite of the trappings of wealth

and family prominence, Lucas fought his inner fears and shortcomings, just as everyone else did. If his strong face had become inexpressibly dear to her during the past few weeks—well, no one would ever know that.

Lucas had pushed the ornate silver pen stand out of his way, replacing it with a laptop computer. At the moment he frowned at the computer screen even while talking with someone on the phone.

He glanced up at the movement of the door and beckoned to her. By the time she'd reached the desk he'd concluded the call and hung up.

"You didn't have to stop what you're doing on my account."

He grimaced. "Nothing important, believe me. Baxter seems to think his empire will collapse because he's bedridden, but everything is ticking along as usual."

"Because you're already running it all." Did he ever long to go off and use those architectural skills doing what he wanted, instead of what Baxter wanted? Probably he didn't let himself think that. His sense of responsibility got in the way.

"I suppose." He leaned back, clearly dismissing the topic. "What can I do for you?"

"Nothing." She shook her head. "I don't mean that to be rude. Just—literally, nothing. I've decided to go home."

That did surprise him. She saw it in his eyes. If he asked her to stay…

But he wouldn't. Whatever they might have felt for each other was impossible, and they both knew it. Lucas's life would be far simpler without her.

"Why have you decided that?" His tone was carefully neutral.

"There's nothing for me here." Saying the words aloud set a seal of finality to them. She managed a smile. "You saw my grandfather's reaction to the wonderful news that I'm related to him. I don't want to cause any more heart attacks."

Lucas pushed his chair back with a sudden movement, standing. "You didn't cause it. He was angry with Trey."

"Angry with Trey for fathering a child by a Wyoming waitress instead of a Savannah aristocrat. That's me, in case you hadn't noticed."

He rounded the desk, reaching out, and for an instant she thought he'd touch her. He stopped short of that. "It still wasn't your fault."

She shrugged. "That doesn't make any difference, does it? I don't belong here, even though I'm Trey's child."

Her rebellious heart wanted him to say she did belong, but she knew he wouldn't. Trey and Gracie's tragedy should be enough warning that two such different worlds couldn't mesh.

"Corrie…"

His eyes darkened, and he did touch her then—just the lightest touch of his fingers to her hand, and she felt it through every cell of her body.

She shook her head slightly. "There isn't anything left to say, Lucas. Let it go."

He drew in a breath. "Maybe there's nothing I can say, but your grandfather wants to talk with you. Will you go in to see him?"

"I'm not sure that's such a good idea. I might upset him again."

"He wouldn't ask if he didn't want to see you." Lucas held out his hand to her. "Please."

She could hardly refuse. Suppressing her doubts, she

nodded. She put her hand in his and let him lead her into the master bedroom.

Some things had been moved around since the previous day—an easy chair drawn toward the window, a table swept of its normal contents and laden with medications and medical paraphernalia. The large, gold-framed mirror above the fireplace reflected the four-poster bed with its deep red hangings, its gray spread drawn back and neatly folded. A uniformed nurse sat in the Queen Anne chair by the window, a colorful fluff of knitting wool in her lap.

Baxter was propped up on pillows, his white hair neat, his pajama shirt buttoned to his throat. His eyes were half-closed, but he opened them as she approached.

She didn't say anything. All the platitudes, the polite questions about how he was feeling, seemed pointless.

"Lucas told you about the DNA." His voice was raspy, but stronger than she'd expected.

She nodded. "He told me." Was he angry with Lucas for spilling the information? She couldn't tell.

"Well? What do you think about that?" He raised himself on his elbows to glare at her.

The nurse, alerted by the movement, started toward him, and he transferred the glare to her. She subsided, sitting on the edge of her chair as if prepared to leap into action at any moment.

"I never doubted it."

He sniffed, but eased back against the pillows. "I was angry with Trey. I guess it's not your fault."

Coming from Baxter, that was absolutely gracious. She wasn't sure what to say in response. Thanks for not blaming me for being born?

Fortunately he didn't seem to expect a response. "I'll

talk to you about him. When I feel better. And Eulalie and Lydia will, too. I'll see to that." His eyes closed, as if he'd exhausted himself.

Maybe confronting his mortality had made a change in Baxter. *Thank You, Lord.*

Baxter's eyes popped open. "Don't run away with the idea I'm going to make you an heiress, or anything like that."

"I don't want anything."

How many times had she said that? It was the one thing that seemed impossible for Baxter to understand. He'd spent his life obsessed with the power his wealth gave him. In the end, he couldn't understand that it had robbed him, too.

His head moved slightly on the pillow, as if to deny her words. "Go away." His voice turned fretful. "Come back tomorrow."

She took a step away from the bed, only realizing when she moved how tense she'd been. She turned away and walked quickly from the room, aware of Lucas close behind her.

When they'd reached the study, she turned to face him. "Are you responsible for the change in his attitude?"

He shrugged. "Maybe in part. The attack frightened him. It made him more willing to listen to me."

"Why did you bother trying?"

He looked startled at the question. "It's only right. You're Trey's child."

"It means I'll be around for a few more days, I guess." She shouldn't be feeling so pleased at the prospect of spending a little more time with him.

"I guess so." His smile warmed her. "I'm glad we're not saying goodbye just yet. But Corrie—" the smile faded

"—you have to realize that this won't necessarily change the way the others view you."

She nodded, wondering exactly what was in his mind. Was he telling her to expect more rudeness, now that they thought she had a legitimate claim to their inheritance? Or was he warning her to be on guard against any further dangerous accidents?

The garden air smelled fresh as Corrie walked down the wrought-iron steps two mornings later. Only a faint heaviness suggested the heat that would come later, and the red geraniums in their earthenware pots still bore a coating of dew.

It was a pleasant change from sitting indoors, waiting for the infrequent summonses to her grandfather's room. They hadn't talked much yet—Baxter was still too weak for that. But he seemed to want to see her. She hadn't realized how stressful it was until Mrs. Andrews had taken a look at her face and told her brusquely to get some fresh air.

Apparently Mrs. Andrews knew about the DNA results. For all Corrie knew, all of Savannah could be buzzing with the news. How would the rest of her relatives take that notoriety?

She honestly didn't care. She'd managed to avoid them, not wanting a confrontation with Baxter so ill.

I don't even like him much, Lord. I think just about every one of his attitudes wrong. But I can't help caring about him. Is that the power of kinship?

At the base of the stairs she froze. The garden door to Eulalie's house clicked, and Deidre walked quickly toward the back gate. She hadn't glanced in Corrie's direction, thank goodness. An encounter with Deidre was not high on her list of priorities.

No sooner had the gate to the alley closed behind Deidre than Eulalie emerged from the house. She glanced around, spotted Corrie and gave a hesitant wave.

A friendly overture? She could hardly turn away, so she walked across the space between the houses to meet Eulalie.

"Have you seen Deidre?" The question came out abruptly, as if Eulalie didn't have time for her usual pleasantries.

"She went out the back gate a few minutes ago. You just missed her."

"Oh, dear. She's gone off without her cell phone, and I know she needs it today."

Eulalie seemed upset out of proportion to the cause, but good manners compelled a response.

"She hasn't been gone long. Would you like me to try and catch her?"

"Would you, dear?" Eulalie thrust the cell phone into her hand. "I told the nurse I'd take over for a few minutes, and I don't want to be late."

"Of course." That's what she got for being polite—an encounter with Deidre.

"Just go out the gate and turn left. Her car is in the first garage on the right." Eulalie was already turning away.

If she were lucky, Deidre would have left. She crossed the garden, went out the gate and headed for the garage that fronted on the alley.

Obviously her luck was out. She spotted the rear bumper of Deidre's car, jutting out of the garage. Why was it taking her so long to leave?

She reached the open bay door, and shock stopped her. Deidre stood inside the shelter of the garage, but she wasn't alone. Judging by the intensity of their kiss, her companion was no stranger.

She took a cautious step back. Deidre would probably rather do without her cell phone than know Corrie had witnessed the scene. Her foot hit a patch of gravel. It made the smallest of sounds, but the couple sprang apart, spinning toward her.

"You! What are you doing here?" Deidre's eyes blazed, and she took an impetuous step toward Corrie, halted by the man's hand on her arm.

"Spying. Guess this is the cousin you told me about, huh?" He slouched toward Corrie, something vaguely menacing in the way his shoulders hunched under the grease-stained T-shirt he wore.

Greasy T-shirt, torn jeans, a cigarette dangling from his fingers—it didn't take a genius to figure out this wasn't someone Eulalie had in mind for her daughter.

She ignored him, focusing on Deidre. "I wasn't spying on you. Your mother asked me to bring you this." She held out the cell phone.

"Looks like Deidre isn't gonna introduce us, sugar. I'm Win." The man stopped in front of her, too close, and the way he looked her up and down made her feel as if she needed some antiseptic soap.

As an attempt to intimidate it wasn't bad, but she was more annoyed than afraid. She looked past him at Deidre. "Do you want this or not?"

Deidre brushed past her boyfriend and snatched the cell phone. "I suppose you can't wait to rush off and tell your brand-new grandfather about this. It might earn you a few extra points in his will."

She fought to control her anger at the constant assumption that she cared about Baxter's money. "Why should I tell him? It's not my concern who you go out with." She spun and stalked off, still feeling the man's inimical gaze on her.

She almost reached the gate before her conscience attacked. Deidre, as annoying as she could be, was younger than she was and her cousin, like it or not. She ought to at least try...

But when she turned around, Deidre's car was swinging out of the garage. Win leaned against the door frame, watching her go. He gave Corrie an insolent stare and then climbed into a red pickup that looked as if it were held together mostly by rust. With a sputter and a gasp, the pickup headed down the alley.

Deidre's romance wasn't her business. She was certainly the last person Deidre would listen to.

But she had a bad feeling about what Cousin Deidre had gotten herself into.

TEN

"Corrie, is something wrong?" Lydia straightened from behind her rosebushes as Corrie came back through the gate.

"No, not at all." *Except that my foolish cousin has gotten herself involved with a creep who has* trouble *written all over him.* "Your roses are lovely." She cupped a delicate yellow rose in her hand.

"Trey told the gardener to put yellow roses around the patio when Baxter signed the house over to him." Lydia shrugged. "I don't know why—maybe they were a favorite of his current girlfriend."

Trey was long gone, but still the yellow roses bloomed. For an instant her heart hurt with it.

Lydia dropped a fresh-cut bloom into the basket she carried. "I had a short visit with Baxter. He asked me to talk to you about Trey."

At least her grandfather seemed to be going through with his promise. "Did you mention that we'd already talked?"

"I decided that what Baxter didn't know wouldn't hurt him."

Corrie returned her smile, the stress she'd felt over Deidre's behavior fading. "Thanks, Lydia. I appreciate it."

Lydia studied her face, much as Mrs. Andrews had done

earlier. "You know what you need—you need to get away for a while. Let's drive over to Tybee Island and take my boat out."

"I should stay, in case my grandfather wants me."

Lydia's lips tightened, as if she felt people catered to Baxter's wants too much. "Just for a couple of hours. The sea air will blow the worries out of your mind."

"I don't know…" Surprising, how attractive it sounded to get away for a bit.

"Are you going out on the boat?" An eager voice interrupted her thoughts. "Can I come?"

Jason skipped over to them, his eyes bright. Lucas was a few steps behind his son. His gaze connected with Corrie's, and he smiled.

"A trip on Lydia's boat? Sounds like a great idea."

Lydia's smile was a bit slow in coming. "Corrie and I were just talking about it. I thought it would do her good to get away from the sickroom for a while."

"It would do us all good." Lucas put his hand on Jason's shoulder. "Sorry—I guess we seem to be inviting ourselves."

"You're always welcome, Lucas. You know that." Lydia's usual brisk tone returned as she stripped off her gardening gloves. "I'll change and meet you at the garage in half an hour, all right?"

Corrie hadn't actually said she was going, but the others seemed to take it for granted. And given Jason's enthusiasm and the warmth of Lucas's smile, she wouldn't miss it for the world.

The drive out to Tybee Island let her see something of Savannah's surrounding area. They took Route 80 out of town, with Lucas pointing out sites of interest as they drove. The road eventually narrowed to a two-lane highway as they approached Tybee Island, passing Fort Pulaski before they reached the bridge.

"If you feel like climbing 178 steps, we can go to the top of the Tybee Island Light," Lucas said, turning off the main road onto a side road that bordered a tidal creek.

"I'm not sure my legs are up to that," she said lightly.

"We can bring Cousin Corrie another day, can't we, Dad?" Jason's sweet smile warmed her. He, at least, accepted her.

Lucas glanced at her, and his smile generated its own brand of warmth. "You bet."

The boat, when they reached it, looked awfully small to Corrie, although Lydia said it was a seventeen-footer. Lydia and Jason scrambled easily from the dock to the boat, heedless of the way the boat rocked. Lydia glanced at her impatiently.

"Come aboard. We have to go while the tide is with us."

Lucas, seeming to sense her hesitation, took her hand. "It's simple," he said quietly. "I'll step in first and hold your hand."

She nodded. Lucas couldn't know, would never know, why the thought of the ocean wrenched at her heart. There was a poem they'd had to learn in junior high, about someone's father lying at the bottom of the ocean, his bones turning to coral. She'd had nightmares for weeks, but it was her mother's face she saw.

She couldn't let them see her feelings. She could balance herself on a galloping horse, couldn't she? A boat should be a cinch in comparison.

Lucas stepped aboard easily. She gripped his hand and negotiated the step from dock to deck, stumbling a little when the boat rocked under her. His firm grip wouldn't let her fall.

"Haven't you ever been on a boat, Cousin Corrie?" Jason asked.

She shook her head. "There's not much call for that where I live." She collapsed thankfully onto the padded bench seat.

Lucas cast off the lines and came to sit next to her as Lydia started the motor and the boat putted slowly out to the center of the channel. Jason stood next to Lydia, talking to her a mile a minute about the boat.

"Odd that you've never been on a boat." Lydia tossed the words over her shoulder, her eyes narrowed against the sunlight. "Trey loved the water—practically grew up on it."

Lydia accelerated then, saving Corrie the trouble of answering.

"We'll go down the channel to the ocean. Have you seen it before?" Lucas's voice was low, under the roar of the boat's engine.

"No." She bit off the word. "I suppose that would have been a disappointment to my father, as well."

Lucas leaned a little closer, his eyes nearly golden in the sunlight. "Corrie, I didn't mean it that way. Lydia didn't either, I'm sure."

She nodded, suppressing the image of bones made of coral. "Sorry. I guess I'm a little sensitive about the reminders of how strange my life has been in comparison to my father's."

"You've had different experiences. Not better or worse, just different."

Lucas was trying to make her feel better, but what did he know about the constant struggle just to maintain a decent standard of living? About the strain of worrying about how her college loans were going to be paid?

Still, that wasn't Lucas's fault. She managed a smile, keeping a firm grip on the handrail of the boat. "I guess you're right."

His fingers closed over hers. "You're holding on to that railing like you're on a roller coaster. Relax. Lydia's an excellent sailor."

"I have every confidence in her." She gritted her teeth as Lydia swung the boat in a wide semicircle, and Corrie realized they were moving out into open water.

"No offense, Lydia." Lucas raised his voice to be heard over the engine. "But I'd rather we put on the life jackets out here."

Lydia nodded, gesturing to a locker opposite them. Corrie's breath caught as Lucas stood and walked unconcernedly across the moving deck. He tossed a child-size life jacket to his son, watching while Jason put it on, and then brought one to Corrie.

He grinned at her, balancing easily against the rocking of the waves. "You'll have to let go of the rail long enough to slip your arm in."

"Okay, I'm a coward about this." She gripped the rail with one hand while she shoved the other arm in and repeated the process. "I confess."

Lucas sat back down beside her. His fingers moved nimbly, fastening the life jacket around her and pulling the straps tight. "It's okay." His fingers brushed her cheek. "You don't have to be a hero about everything. It's okay to be afraid of the water."

"Not the water." She frowned, keeping her gaze on a pelican as it dived toward the waves. "I mean, I enjoy swimming. It's just the idea of all that expanse of ocean." She nodded toward the open water that seemed to stretch into infinity.

Full fathom five thy father lies— The poem must have engraved its way into her memory.

Lucas settled a bit closer—close enough that she could feel the warmth of his body, could sense the strength in the arm he put casually around her.

"I guess it does seem scary the first time you see it."

He was being kind, but he didn't understand. He couldn't. Bile was rising in her throat, and she forced it down. She wouldn't be sick in front of them.

Jason still stood next to Lydia. They'd never hear her quiet words with the roar of the engine.

"I've dreamed about it. Often." She didn't know she was going to tell him until the words were on her lips. "My mother drowned in the ocean."

She felt, rather than heard, his sharp intake of breath.

"I didn't know. I'm sorry. You said she died in an accident—I guess I was thinking a car accident."

She blinked at the sudden rush of tears in her eyes. Why would she cry? It wasn't as if she'd ever known her mother.

"Did it happen—" He stopped, and she could almost hear the wheels turning. "Where did it happen? You said you were only six months old when she died on a trip back to Savannah."

She nodded, carefully editing her words. Maybe she could trust him, but she wasn't going to. Some things were better left unsaid.

"She told my aunt she was coming here, to see Baxter. She called once, just to say she was on her way. My aunt didn't hear anything else until she learned that my mother's car had been found abandoned on a beach down near Jacksonville, Florida. Her body was never recovered."

He seemed to be trying to make sense of it. "Surely there must have been an investigation. What was she doing there if she was coming to Savannah?"

"I don't know. It doesn't make much sense." So much she didn't know, she'd never know. "I found a report the police in Florida sent to my aunt. Her car was found on a deserted beach, with all her things intact. It looked as if she'd just parked and gone for a swim. There was no sign of foul play. Nothing to investigate. They thought she didn't understand the tides and was swept out in the current."

"Your aunt didn't look into it any further? Go herself?"

Anger flickered through her, raw with pain. "How could she? She had little enough money and a baby to support. She'd never been out of Wyoming in her life. What would you expect her to do?" She shook her head, blinking back tears. She'd never thought she'd tell him that much. He wouldn't understand.

And she'd never tell anyone the rest of it.

Corrie was holding something back, Lucas was sure. After spilling that shocking secret on the boat, she'd forced the conversation into other channels. She'd talked brightly about the sights—too brightly. That glitter in her eyes wasn't pleasure. If anything, it signaled suppressed tears.

How could he understand her so well in such a short period of time? It was as if he could see right past her beautiful face to her soul.

He backed away from that thought as soon as it occurred. He couldn't know her that well. And he couldn't ask what she was holding back, because to do so would assume that they had a deeper relationship than was possible.

Eventually Corrie would leave. She'd go back to the life that satisfied her, and he'd continue to do his duty. That was the future, and he didn't see a way of changing it. Didn't want to change it.

So he kept his peace, and pointed out the brown pelicans that dived for their food, the squawking gulls, the fishing boats, the slender shaft of the Tybee Island Light. And when they'd docked, driven home and they walked back through the gate to the garden, he seemed to feel the walls close around him.

They'd just stepped inside when he saw Ainsley come barreling toward them, clearly upset. His heart clenched. Trouble.

"Ainsley, what's wrong? Is it Baxter?" If Baxter had taken a turn for the worse while they were out, he wouldn't easily forgive himself.

Ainsley stopped short, his fists clenching. "Baxter? Oh, Baxter's fine. He's well enough to threaten to disinherit me. Seemed to perk him up no end, as a matter of fact."

"What on earth are you talking about?" He shouldn't have left, obviously. Eulalie hadn't the wit to keep the two of them separated. "Don't you have sense enough to avoid explosive subjects when your great-uncle is ill?"

"Me?" Ainsley flung out his hand dramatically. "I didn't bring anything up. He sent for me, because he knows." He glared at Corrie. "He knows because you told him."

"I didn't," Corrie said quickly. "I didn't tell him a thing about it, honestly."

Lucas gritted his teeth. "Corrie, you're beginning to sound as overwrought as your cousins. Obviously the two of you know what you're talking about, but I don't. Please explain."

"You did." Ainsley ignored him. "No one else knew about it, so no one else could have told him."

"I think we'll skip this," Lydia said, her tone as calm as ever. She took Jason's hand. "Come along, Jason. I have some oatmeal raisin cookies in my cookie jar."

Lucas gave her a thankful nod. You could always count on Lydia to behave sensibly. Jason didn't need to hear his elders behaving badly.

He waited until the two of them were out of earshot and then turned back to Ainsley. "Now. Stop ranting and tell me exactly what it is you imagine Corrie has told Baxter about you."

Ainsley gave him a sulky frown, looking about twelve. Sometimes it was impossible to believe he was a man instead of a boy.

"I'm designing the sets for an experimental theater company. Corrie was spying on me, and—"

"I was not spying on you!"

Lucas held up his hand, silencing Corrie. Obviously he was back to his usual family role—the buffer who had to keep the peace at all costs.

"How did you find out?"

Corrie took a breath at his calm tone, seeming to force down her anger. "I was walking back from having lunch with Lydia when I saw Ainsley going into the theater building. Why would I spy on him? There's nothing wrong with what he's doing."

"Unfortunately Baxter wouldn't see it that way." He looked at Ainsley, who wouldn't meet his gaze. "I take it this is what you've been doing on all those long lunch hours of yours."

"I might as well." Ainsley flared up, his cheeks flushing. "I'm no good at the office—we both know that. But you know what Uncle Baxter is like. Everyone has to do exactly what he thinks is best. I'm tired of it."

"Why don't you stand up for yourself, then?" Corrie planted her fists on her hips as if ready to do just that. "I didn't tell him because I promised I wouldn't, but I don't understand what all the fuss is about."

"Of course you told him. Why not? Now that you've proved you're Trey's daughter, you're ready to get rid of the competition. Have you suggested that Baxter rewrite his will yet?"

"You people are obsessed with that. How many times do I have to tell you that I didn't come here because I wanted a piece of your pie? I have a perfectly good life in Wyoming, and I don't want anything from my grandfather."

"Oh, that's rich. Sure, you're going to go back to running a café and living on food stamps."

"I do not live on food stamps!"

Corrie's cheeks were scarlet. He'd best intervene before this got any worse.

If Ainsley really were twelve, he'd send him to his room. "Ainsley, you're behaving badly, and you know it. You also know that Baxter will cool off. He's not going to disinherit you."

"Really?" Ainsley flung out his hand toward Corrie. "Wake up and smell the coffee. Here's Trey's replacement, the new favorite child. She'll have all of us out on the street before she's done."

"That's ridiculous," he said sharply.

"Is it?" Ainsley's eyes glittered. "Tell me this, Lucas. How are you going to feel when Baxter leaves the company you've spent your life building to Corrie?"

Corrie stood staring as Ainsley charged out of the garden after delivering his bombshell. For a moment she couldn't look at Lucas, afraid of what she might see on his face.

But that was ridiculous. She knew what kind of man

Lucas was after the time they'd spent together. He wouldn't react to a childish challenge thrown out in a fit of spite.

She turned toward him, trying to smile. "Lucas, I'm sorry you got dragged into that. But honestly, I didn't spill Ainsley's secret."

She hoped he would join her in smiling at Ainsley's behavior. Instead, his face seemed to lock down, turning into that charming mask that didn't let anyone in.

"Don't worry about it, Corrie. Ainsley overreacts to everything. I'll talk to Baxter and straighten it out."

"What he said about the company—Baxter wouldn't do that."

His mouth might have tightened infinitesimally. That was all the emotion she could read. "Baxter can do what he likes with what he owns. He doesn't owe me anything."

"But he does. You run everything for him, besides trying to keep peace in the family." She'd feel a lot better if he'd just react in some way.

Lucas just shrugged. "I don't think Baxter sees it that way. In any event, it doesn't matter."

"It does to me." She put her hand on his arm, but it was like iron, hard and unforgiving. "If he tried to do that, I wouldn't take anything from him."

He pulled away, still giving her that polite smile. "Forget it, Corrie. The situation will work itself out. Now, speaking of work, I have some things to check on. Excuse me."

He walked off quickly, and all she could do was watch him go and think that she should have handled the situation better.

I don't understand these people, Father. Each time I think I'm getting closer, something happens to push me away. Help me see more clearly what You want me to do.

She pushed her windblown hair out of her face. Well, like it or not, what she should do was check on her grandfather. If he seemed strong enough to talk, she'd try once again to make him understand that she didn't want anything from him.

She crossed quickly to Baxter's house, up the wrought-iron stairs, and into the quiet hallway. No matter how long she stayed here, she'd never get used to the silence. The house felt more like a museum than a home. Had Trey ever slid down the polished railing or bounced a basketball on the Oriental carpets? She still couldn't imagine what it had been like to grow up here.

Upstairs, she found the door to her grandfather's bedroom standing ajar. She pushed it open, catching the nurse's eye.

The woman put her finger to her lips, shaking her head. Corrie nodded, backing out soundlessly.

"Is that Corrie?" Baxter's voice sounded querulous, but stronger than it had earlier. "Tell her to come in. I want to see her."

Shrugging, the nurse beckoned to her. She went inside, crossing to the upholstered chair that had been set next to the bed. Ainsley had probably sat there when he'd been summoned to the room to be grilled about his misdeeds. Exasperated as she was with Ainsley, she suspected his mother and his great-uncle were more to blame than he was for his problems. Maybe, if Baxter seemed well enough, she should ask him how he'd found out about Ainsley.

"How are you feeling?" She sat on the edge of the seat, prepared to make a fast exit if he seemed too tired to talk.

"Fine, fine." He waved the nurse away irritably. "Go take a coffee break or something. I want to talk to my granddaughter alone."

Her heart seemed to contract. That was probably the first time he'd referred to her as his granddaughter.

The woman faded quietly from the room. Baxter turned his head restlessly on the pillow. "I have something for you." He pointed to an object on the bedside table. "Go ahead, take it."

She picked it up. "A photo album." She shot a questioning glance at him. "Are these of Trey?"

He nodded. "I thought you should see them. Eulalie probably has more. She was always taking pictures, half of them out of focus."

She opened the album's burgundy leather cover. Thick creamy pages held the photos—studio pictures. The first one was of a baby, dressed in a christening gown, all lace and ruffles. The round face stared solemnly out at her.

"Is this my father?"

"He hated that picture when he got older. Wanted to know what we meant by dressing him up like a china doll." He made a wheezing noise that might have been a laugh. "My wife's idea. That gown had come down through her family, and she said she'd use it for all our children." His fingers moved, plucking at the bedspread. "But we had only one."

Her throat tightened. Baxter had revealed more about himself in those few sentences than he had in everything else he'd said to her. That sense of longing, of loss—it came through so clearly, but he'd resent it if she betrayed that she'd heard it.

"It's nice to have an heirloom like that for a baptism. I wore a dress that had been my mother's. My great-aunt saved it for me."

He shifted his position slightly. "Well, go on. Look at the rest. Ask me any questions you want."

She paged through the pictures—Trey at one, teetering proudly on his own two feet; Trey as a toddler, pulling a toy across a polished floor. She stopped at one of him on a swing, his head tilted so that the sunlight touched his blond curls.

Her throat tightened so that it would have been difficult to speak. She hadn't thought about looking like him, but something in the tilt of the head, the curve of his smile, reminded her irresistibly of a photo of her at that age.

"What's wrong?" Baxter's voice was gruff.

"Nothing. I guess…" She stopped, not sure how honest to be with him. "I think I see a resemblance."

He tilted the album to see which picture she was looking at. "Yes." He grated the word. "I saw that. That's why it doesn't matter how sure the DNA experts are. I knew."

He knew. How long had he been sure she was Trey's child? From the beginning? Surely not.

She resisted the urge to ask him. Upsetting him was the last thing she wanted to do. But she had to make him see that it was wrong to taunt the others over the possibility of making her his heir. Even if that upset him, she had to try. She turned a page.

"That was his first sailboat." Baxter pushed himself higher on the pillow. "He was a natural. Did well at any sport he tried." He gave that rasping laugh again. "His mother said he was like me. You'd never guess it now, but I was quite an athlete in my day."

"I believe you. You probably did anything you set your mind to."

When had the trouble started between him and Trey? Once his wife was no longer around to serve as a buffer between them?

She turned another page—Trey in a suit and tie, a pretty girl on his arm, headed to a school dance, probably.

"Could have had any girl he wanted."

She closed the album, knowing where that was headed. "You're getting tired. Maybe we can finish looking at them another time."

"You take it." He turned his head away, as if the journey into the past had exhausted him. "I don't need to look at pictures of him. He failed me."

She remembered Lydia's story of his intent to destroy the portrait out of what? Grief? Anger? Guilt? No one knew but Baxter.

She closed the album carefully. "Since you feel that way, you'll understand why I don't want anything from you."

He didn't move for a moment. Then his face turned toward her, his eyes like blue ice. "What are you talking about?"

She quailed inside at the intensity of that look, but she wouldn't let him see it. "You have the others upset about whether you might change your will. I don't want anything."

Color rushed into his face, frightening her more than his pallor had. "Did they send you in here to talk to me?"

"No, of course not." Good work, Corrie. You've just made it worse. "I just want to be clear that I don't want—"

He cut her off with a sharp gesture. "Don't try to delude me. You want it. You're just like your mother. She was going to take money from me to leave Trey." His hand shook, and his breath wheezed. "But I didn't have to pay her. He died."

ELEVEN

Corrie sat alone in the garden, where Lucas had expected her to be. She perched on the rim of the fountain, hand moving slowly through the water. Did she even realize how much she seemed to need that contact with nature in this alien setting?

Worse than alien—hostile. He'd stepped into Baxter's room to get him up to date on the latest construction project, only to hear what had probably been a biased account of her conversation with her grandfather. Frustration tightened his jaw until his teeth ached. Did Baxter really think he'd forge a relationship with his granddaughter by insulting her mother?

Judging by the lost look on Corrie's face, she wasn't dealing with Baxter's revelation well. The longing he felt to comfort her startled him with its strength. He wasn't sure he could, but he had to try.

She looked up at his approach, and the way she forced a smile told him that she wasn't ready to share this problem with him.

"Are you back from your round of the businesses?"

He nodded, sitting beside her on the fountain's wall. "As you see. How have things been here? Any further explosions?"

It was an opening for her to tell him what Baxter had said. But she just shook her head.

"Fairly quiet. I haven't seen Ainsley since he stormed out." Two fine lines formed between her brows. "I didn't handle that well. I just wish I could convince him that I didn't spill his secret."

She was worried about Ainsley, who hadn't done anything that he could see to earn her friendship. "Ainsley was kidding himself if he thought Baxter wouldn't find out. Savannah's really a small town at heart. Despite what Ainsley thinks, there are probably a hundred people who could have mentioned it."

That didn't seem to comfort her. He stood up abruptly. She looked up at him, eyes widening.

"Is something wrong?"

"No. Just—" He held out his hand. "Will you come with me? There's something I'd like to show you."

She hesitated for a second and then nodded. "All right."

She may have been surprised when he led her out of the garden and down to the garage, but she didn't object. It wasn't until they'd pulled out into traffic that she raised her eyebrows.

"Now can I know where we're going?"

"The church. It occurs to me that I haven't really made good on my promise to help you learn more about your father. That's a good place to start."

By the time they'd parked and made their way into the silent sanctuary, he'd begun to wonder if this was such a good idea. Still, Corrie couldn't evade the fact of her father's death. The last time they were in the church, he hadn't been convinced of her identity. Now he was, and she should be shown what there was to see of her family here.

She stood for a moment, looking down the wide center aisle. Slanting sunlight from the stained glass windows laid patterns of crimson and gold across the pews. "It's a beautiful sanctuary. But what does it have to tell me about my father?"

He touched her arm, leading her toward the side aisle. "The Mannings have worshipped here since the church was built. Trey grew up in this church—attended church school classes, was confirmed, sat in the same pew every Sunday." He gestured. "I suppose he must have looked at this a few thousand times."

The stained glass window soared above them, its rich jewel tones highlighting the scriptural scene.

"It's beautiful." Corrie took a step back to see the window more fully. "Jesus with Mary and Martha, isn't it?"

He nodded toward the inscription at the bottom.

"In loving memory of Mary Elizabeth Manning," Corrie read. "A relative?"

"Baxter's mother. He commissioned it as a memorial. It was part of Trey's history, and it's part of yours, too."

Something crossed her face that might have been sorrow. "I wish…"

"What?" he asked, when she didn't go on.

She shrugged. "It just made me think that I'd like to give something to my church in memory of my great-aunt. I'm afraid my funds don't run to stained glass windows, though."

He leaned against the windowsill. "She brought you up in the church, did she?"

Corrie's smile flickered. "She was a strong Christian woman who never took excuses for doing less than your best. I wish you could have known her."

"She sounds like my grandmother. 'Obedience is better than sacrifice' was her favorite scripture."

"Maybe they had something in common." She sounded a little surprised. "What about your family? Did you attend here, too?"

"Oh, yes. My parents were married here. And buried from here."

"I'm sorry."

He shrugged. "They were sweethearts from the time they were children. Neither of them would have wanted to go on alone." He wondered, sometimes, whether his parents' deaths in the plane crash had helped push him into marriage. He'd been lost without them, but that wasn't a good enough reason for marrying.

"I wish I had memories of my parents."

It shook him then—the realization that she had no memories at all. He'd at least had twenty-four years of memories to sustain him. He touched the brass plaque mounted on the wall beneath the window.

"This is in memory of Trey."

Corrie reached out to trace the name and the dates with her fingertips. "I didn't notice it on Sunday." A shiver went through her. "My mother's name isn't here."

"No." He didn't know quite what to say. "I suppose Baxter felt—"

"I know what Baxter felt." Her anger flared. "He's made it quite clear what he thought of my mother. He said that she was going to take money from him to go away."

"Corrie—" What could he say? He didn't have the words to comfort her. "She was very young, and apparently very unhappy."

"So of course you accept that. Well, I don't. Either

he's lying, or he's wrong. I don't believe she would have done that."

"You never knew her, Corrie." He kept his voice gentle.

"I know." Her anger scorched. "She was kind and gentle, and she loved Trey enough to leave everything for him. If his family hadn't gotten in the way, they could have been happy."

"You make them sound like Romeo and Juliet." And if she went on thinking of them in that way, she was bound to be hurt.

"Maybe I do. Maybe that's who they were." She rubbed her arms, as if suddenly cold. "Other people couldn't accept their love. They died."

"Don't try to lay blame." His voice was sharper than he intended, but he didn't want her to walk into more grief. "You don't know enough to do that, and maybe you never will."

Her chin came up, her eyes bright with anger. "You're not a very good person to preach about blaming," she shot back. "You blame yourself every day of your life for your wife's death."

He could only stare at her, feeling the truth go straight to his heart. Corrie was right. His guilt was running his life. And there wasn't a thing he could do about it.

Six in the morning was the only time it was reasonable to jog in Savannah, Corrie had decided. She rounded the corner by City Market, sweat trickling down her back under her T-shirt. Even at this hour, the humid air stuck to her like glue.

After everything that had happened the previous day, she'd needed a good long run to clear her head. Not that it felt much clearer. Baxter's words when he'd denounced her mother; Lucas's eyes when she'd struck out at him—both those things would take more than a run to clear away.

Her feet thudded on the pavement in time to the beating of her heart. She turned the corner into the alley, welcoming the shade from the buildings on either side. Pickup trucks were pulled up to the back doors of restaurants, unloading produce fresh from the farms, probably picked before the sun was up this morning.

She jogged down the center of the alley, dodging a stream of water from a man hosing off the back stoop of a restaurant. He gave her a friendly wave before turning back to his cleaning, probably finding her a familiar sight by now, since she'd come this way every morning this week.

If she stopped clinging to her defenses, maybe she could think straight about everything that had been happening. Lucas hadn't been derisive when he'd said she was thinking of her parents as Romeo and Juliet. He'd probably been attempting to be kind.

But what did he expect? Of course she idealized her parents. That was normal enough, surely. If they'd lived, if they'd stayed together, she'd have gone through the usual adolescent stage of hating them, probably, knowing it was safe to do so because nothing could make them stop loving her.

She slowed to cross the street and jogged across it into the next alley. This alley lacked the life and energy of the previous block. Tall narrow buildings turned their backs on the alleyway, not even dignifying it with a trash can or two. It was an unexpectedly deserted area in the middle of the city, but at its far end, it came out a short distance from the garage and the back gate into the garden. By the time she got there, she'd be ready for a quick shower and one of the gargantuan breakfasts Mrs. Andrews insisted on serving.

The rumble of a motor announced that a car had pulled

into the alley behind her. She edged toward the side, leaving him room to pass.

Maybe she'd have a chance to see Lucas this morning. At the very least, she owed him an apology for her anger. He'd just been trying to help.

The vehicle behind had slowed, apparently unwilling to pass her in the narrow confines. She turned, intending to gesture him past.

It wasn't a car, but a pickup—maybe one of the farm pickups that had been dropping off produce. She swung her arm, indicating that there was room to pass her. Odd, the way he hung back. Sunlight glinted off a dusty windshield, making it impossible to see the driver.

Well, if he wanted to stay behind her all the way to the street that was his problem. She jogged on another few feet. Then she heard it. The roar of acceleration echoed, bouncing crazily off blank walls.

She shot one startled, frightened glance behind her. The truck was coming at her, gaining speed, looking for all the world as if the driver intended to plough right into her. She picked up speed, veering sharply to the side to let him pass.

But he wasn't attempting to pass. He was aiming the car at her like a gun.

Her heart pounded. Shelter—she had to have shelter, but there was nothing along the alley, nothing but blank facades and locked doors, no sign of life, no one to help her....

Seconds, she had seconds before he hit her. *Please, God, please—*

A railing ahead—a metal railing fencing in a stairwell that descended to basement level. If she could reach that—

She put on a burst of speed, forcing her aching legs to

pump, her gasping lungs to pull in another breath of air. Don't think, don't turn, don't look, just race for the railing, grab it, vault over and pray—

The pickup screamed past, its rear panel scraping the metal railing. She huddled in the cellar-way, hands over her head, waiting.

Then he was gone, and the alley was still, the only sound her muffled gasps.

Thank You, Lord. Thank You. She was still in one piece, more or less. She started up the concrete steps, wincing as her right knee bent. Her running pants were shredded and filthy, and blood trickled down her leg.

But she was all right. She stumbled up the steps, hobbling as a fresh spurt of pain hit her knee. Not too bad. She'd be able to make it back to the house.

She stopped at the corner, looking cautiously both ways before limping across the street. There was the garage, beyond it the gate to the garden. She'd go in, clean up, and no one would be the wiser.

And then she and Deidre were going to have a little talk. She'd caught a glimpse of the truck from her shelter in the stairwell. It had been a dusty, rusty red pickup, just like the one Deidre's boyfriend drove.

"Corrie? What happened?" Lucas stopped between the gate and the garage, briefcase in hand, obviously on his way to the office.

"Nothing. I'm fine." Well, he wasn't going to believe that, not with blood trickling down her leg.

"You're not fine." His arm went around her quickly. "You're been in an accident."

Another accident, was that what he was thinking? Savannah didn't seem especially healthy for her.

"A truck driver didn't want to share the alley with a jogger, I guess. I had to dive for cover or be a hood ornament."

"Did you get the number?" He half led, half carried her to the gate. "I'll call the police."

She opened her mouth to tell him and closed it again. If it had been Deidre's boyfriend, what then? Did she really want to open that can of worms with the police? Maybe she was getting as bad as the rest of them about the sanctity of the family name, but she didn't think so.

"Sorry, I didn't. I was too busy cowering in a filthy cellar-way."

"The doctor, then. He'll be coming to check on Baxter anyway."

It was tempting, very tempting, to keep leaning on him. To let Lucas do what he did best—take care of people. But she wasn't one of his dependents, and playing the fainting damsel in distress wasn't exactly her style.

"I'm fine, Lucas. Really." She managed a smile at his worried look. "All I need is a shower and a little antiseptic."

He opened the garden door and helped her inside. "At least take the elevator up."

"I will. Go on to work, now. I don't need any nursing."

He stood looking down at her for a moment—just long enough for her to remember what he'd confided about his wife and to wish she'd bitten her tongue before she'd let that come out.

But he didn't look as if he'd taken offense. He just looked as if he cared.

He touched her cheek lightly in the smallest caress. "Take care of yourself, Corrie." His voice was very soft. "We can't afford to lose you."

And then he turned and was gone, leaving her with scarlet cheeks and the feeling that it was her heart he'd touched.

The garage wasn't the most pleasant place to wait for Deidre, but Corrie was determined to catch her alone. Deidre should arrive home from work soon, and Corrie didn't want an audience for the conversation they were about to have.

Sure enough, Deidre's car pulled into the garage before she'd stood there for more than five minutes. A good thing, since at the rate she was stiffening up, she wouldn't have been able to walk if she'd waited any longer. She pushed away from the wall.

A variety of expressions raced across Deidre's face, and she brushed back a wing of dark, wiry hair with a hand that wasn't quite steady. "Corrie, you startled me. What are you doing here?"

"Waiting for you. We have to talk."

Deidre's pointed chin lifted. "I don't have anything to say to you."

"Fine, then I'll talk. Why did you sic your boyfriend on me?"

"I don't know what you're talking about." The words were quick—too quick.

"Get serious, Deidre. Didn't you realize I'd recognize his truck? Or did you hope I'd be dead?"

That got her attention. She stared at Corrie, eyes wide. "Dead? He wasn't supposed to—"

"Kill me? What do you think happens when a couple of tons of metal connects with an unprotected human body?" She caught Deidre's arm, refusing to let her turn away.

"Win wouldn't. He couldn't." But fear threaded her voice.

"Win tried to run me down in an alley with his truck." She had to be blunt to break through Deidre's denial. "He picked a good spot—no witnesses, nowhere to run. If I hadn't tumbled down a cellar-way, I'd be lucky to be alive."

Now it was Deidre's fingers that clutched her arm. "Are you all right?" There was no mistaking the panic.

"Bruises, cuts, a ruined pair of running pants." She forced the words out lightly, because if she thought too much about those moments, she'd start to shake all over again. "Did you set him up to do it along with pushing me off the curb and following me on the street that night?"

"No!" Her grip tightened. "Corrie, you have to believe me. I didn't mean—nothing was supposed to happen. He was just supposed to scare you so you'd leave."

"Deidre…" What could she say that would make her see how dangerous a game she was playing? "I know you're unhappy with your life, but he isn't the answer. Win isn't somebody you can control. If you keep on the way you're going, you'll be the one to get hurt."

"Win would never hurt me." She jerked away from Corrie. "You're lying about this. You must be."

"What's she lying about, baby?" Win's voice had them both turning toward the bay door. He sauntered in, eyes narrowed.

"She said you tried to run her down. You didn't, did you?"

"She's a liar, you know that. Sneaking in here, trying to get in line for the money." His face darkened, and Corrie could almost see the rage boiling beneath the surface. "You're not going to believe her, are you?"

Corrie limped a step to the workbench that stood against the wall. No sensible person would try anything in broad daylight, but she suspected common sense wasn't one of Win's qualities. Her hand closed over a nice, heavy wrench.

Deidre stared at him for a long moment. Corrie couldn't see her expression, but tension stiffened every line of her body.

He held out his hand to her. "Come on, baby. You trust me, don't you?"

"No." The word dragged out of her. "You did it, didn't you? You tried to run over Corrie." She no longer sounded as if she hoped he would deny it.

Anger flashed in his face. "You siding with her against me?"

"Go away, Win." Deidre seemed to sag into herself. "Just get away from me."

Corrie saw the rage flood through him, saw his hand form a fist. Before he could move, she did, lifting the wrench so he could see it.

"You think you can stop me?"

"I'd be glad to give it a try." She hefted the wrench, praying she wouldn't have to use it. "Get out, Win. I haven't called the cops yet, but I will if I see you near either of us again."

For an instant the outcome hung in the balance. Her muscles trembled with the effort of holding up the heavy wrench.

Please, Lord.

Then, with a muttered obscenity, he spun and stalked to his truck. He roared off down the alley.

Corrie dropped the wrench, bending over to catch her breath. When she looked up, Deidre was staring at her.

"Would you really have gone after him with that?"

"If he'd tried to hurt either one of us, you bet I would." A shudder bent through her. "I never thought—" A sob choked off the words. "I wish you'd never come here!" she shouted, and ran off toward the house.

"That wasn't a very grateful response." Lucas stepped around the corner of the garage.

For an instant she was speechless at his sudden appearance. She leaned back against the car, hoping he couldn't see that every muscle trembled, and tried for a normal tone. "She has to blame somebody, I guess. How long have you been here?"

He came toward her. "About as long as you have. I didn't want to interfere, but I was worried about you. I knew there was more to your accident than you told me."

Anger spurted. "I trust you might have interfered if I'd had to use the wrench," she snapped.

"I would have." He studied her gravely. "It occurred to me that for once, Deidre should have to face the consequences of her actions."

The anger ebbed away. He was, as always, doing what he thought best for everyone. "I hope it makes her see some sense." She looked down at the wrench on the concrete. "I'd pick that up, but if I got down there, I might not get up again."

"I've got it." He grabbed the wrench and put it on the workbench, then braced his hands against the rough wood. "I guess we know now who's to blame for all the accidents that have happened to you here. Deidre's friend. Do you want to call the police?"

She shook her head, so tired even that was an effort. "And expose Deidre's part in it? I may not have much family feeling, but I won't do that."

At least now she didn't have to see danger in every shadow. Win was essentially a coward. He wouldn't come back.

"Deidre's been given everything except the chance to

prove herself as a person. I never saw that, until you came."
Lucas's gaze was so warm she seemed to feel it on her skin.

"I don't think Deidre wants to model herself on me. She's not a bad kid. We might even be friends, if she could get over the idea that I want to take what's hers."

His face darkened suddenly. "This is Baxter's doing. He should let go of the reins and tell them where they stand."

"Do you think he's likely to do that?"

"No." He bit off the word. "But he should, before there's real trouble."

TWELVE

"Where's Ainsley? I haven't seen the boy in days." The question, inserted curtly into the middle of a business discussion, took Lucas by surprise.

He eyed Baxter cautiously. After several days of bed rest, the old man looked better—his skin was no longer the color of aged parchment, and his eyes had regained some of their zest. Still, discretion was probably advisable.

"I haven't seen much of him, either. I understand he's been busy with his reenactors' unit, practicing for the Civil War encampment. That's this weekend."

"Nothing wrong with my memory," Baxter snarled, somewhat inaccurately, since he'd clearly forgotten the event. "Well, at least that shows he has some pride in his heritage."

"Of course," he murmured, although he wasn't sure his heritage was the primary reason Ainsley liked to wear a confederate uniform and sport a saber. It was the acting and pageantry Ainsley loved.

"Better than that theater nonsense, anyway." Baxter gave him a sharp look. "Don't tell me you approved of that."

"It's not my business to approve or disapprove of Ainsley's hobbies," he said neutrally. "He's grown now."

"Meaning, it's not my business, either, I suppose." Baxter gave a crack of laughter. "Never mind being tactful. You think I handle that boy all wrong."

"Meaning I think a little tact on your part would ease the tension around here. Who told you about the theater?"

"Lydia, I think. Ran across it on one of her interminable committees. Why?"

"I just wondered." There was no point in saying Ainsley blamed Corrie. Baxter would probably be happy to add fuel to the fire.

Ainsley had been staying out of the way as much as possible, and Deidre seemed to be making an effort to get along with Corrie. Still, the tension was there, and he didn't like it. The atmosphere felt as if a storm were brewing, and he wasn't sure from which direction that storm was coming.

"They'd think I was dying if I started being tactful now." Baxter moved restlessly. He was allowed to sit in his armchair now for periods of time, but that wasn't enough to keep him happy.

He probably shouldn't bring this up, but he was going to. "Are you going to make Corrie an allowance?"

Baxter glared. "Why should I do that?"

"She's your granddaughter."

"Maybe she's better off if she doesn't start depending on me. Besides, she seems to like being independent."

"Yes, she does." It was one of the things he found to admire in Corrie. "But she's Trey's child. You ought to recognize that in your will, at least."

Now he'd managed to raise Baxter's hackles. The old man stiffened, his blue eyes frosty. "It's nobody's business how I leave my property."

Usually he'd soothe Baxter down at a comment like

that, but he suddenly realized how tired he was of always being the buffer in the family. "It's time you told everyone exactly where they stand. And it's also high time you let them do what they want."

Baxter's eyes narrowed. "Are you sure you're not worried about your own inheritance? Afraid I might leave the company to Corrie instead of to you?"

He hadn't liked it when he'd heard that from Ainsley. He liked it even less coming from Baxter.

"If you do, I have other options." He didn't need to add that he'd been offered partnerships in two of the best architectural firms in the city. Baxter knew that.

"Well, you don't need to take me up so sharply." Baxter leaned back in the chair, his tone peevish. "I didn't mean anything. You ought to know by now how much I rely on you."

Regret swept through Lucas. He shouldn't be confronting Baxter when he was ill, even though that illness made these issues even more pressing.

"I know." He put his hand over Baxter's where it lay, thin and lax, on the padded arm of the chair. "You can count on me. I'll take care of things for you."

Baxter nodded, leaning back, eyes closing. His usually neat white hair stood up in a little ruffle on top of his head, and the sign of weakness touched Lucas's heart.

"Do you want me to call the nurse to help you back into bed?"

"In a minute." He opened his eyes to glare at Lucas. "One more thing I need to say to you."

"It can wait."

"No, it can't." He gripped Lucas's arm with something of his old energy. "You know what I want you to do. What will ensure that the company goes to you and your son when I'm gone."

A wave of distaste swept through him. "I've already told you I won't do that."

"It's the least you can do after all that I've done for you."

He stood, Baxter's hand dropping away. "It always comes back to this, doesn't it? You have to have your own way about everything. Not this time. Not for anything you could offer me."

He turned and stalked toward the door, realizing too late that Corrie stood there, her eyes wide and shocked. He brushed by her, but she turned back into the study behind him and closed the door. Her voice stopped him before the wave of anger carried him to the hallway.

"What was that all about?"

He turned, hand braced against the door frame. He could say it wasn't her business, but they'd gone past that stage. Besides, she may as well know what dealing with Baxter was like, just in case she still had any illusions.

"That was about the price tag Baxter's put on leaving me a share of the company I helped build. He wants me to take the Manning name." A fresh wave of anger swept through him. Baxter, in his need to have someone to carry on his family name, seemed to forget that the Santee name meant something, too. "I won't do it. No matter what it costs me."

He slammed out of the room.

As far as Corrie could tell, they didn't need to go to some sort of reenactment—there was enough of a civil war taking place right in the Manning compound. However, she hadn't seen any graceful way out of participating. The entire clan, except for Baxter, was going to support Ainsley.

So here she was, bright and early on Saturday morning, climbing out of Lucas's car into a long, grassy field parked with vehicles of every description. Well, this would be something she'd never done before. She clutched her camera. Nobody back home would believe this if she didn't bring pictures.

And if by attending she managed to mend fences with Ainsley, that was all to the good. She hadn't talked to him in several days, so she hadn't been able to relay what Lucas had passed on—that it was Lydia who'd spilled his secret.

Jason slid out of the car as soon as it was parked. Lucas grabbed him before he could dart off.

"Sunscreen and insect repellent." Lucas handed him the bottles. "And give them to Cousin Corrie when you're done."

Jason applied lotions in a slapdash manner and then raced after Eulalie and Deidre, who had started walking toward the trees. Apparently the actual encampment was farther on.

Corrie eyed Lucas cautiously. It was the first time they'd been alone in a couple of days. Had he been avoiding her since blurting out his anger with her grandfather?

Well, she wasn't one to avoid a difficult subject. "Have you had any more fireworks with Baxter over the name business?"

"No." The word came out curtly. Too curtly. He seemed to realize that, and he shook his head with a slight smile. "I shouldn't have said anything to you about it. I apologize."

"You don't need to apologize." She fell into step with him as they followed the others. "Baxter was out of line."

He darted a sideways glance at her. "You think that?"

"Of course." She shrugged. "You have to admit, it's funny. I have every right to be Corrie Manning if I want to, and he's never said a thing about it. I guess a female doesn't count in his mind."

"Baxter belongs to another century. Speaking of which…" He stopped, gesturing.

They emerged from the trees, and Corrie gasped at the panorama that spread in front of them. Pale canvas tents stood in long, neat rows, and smoke from cooking fires drifted into the air. Around the tents moved a few men in uniform, women in long dresses, even children in period dress.

"I never expected anything like this. It's huge." Beyond the tents, horses were tethered to a line rigged between trees. A rickety spring wagon, pulled by a pair of horses, moved down the row of tents as if it were a street in a town. "You're right—it's like walking into another century."

"Ainsley's unit does it up right." There was a proprietary air to his words that gave him away.

"You're involved in this, too, aren't you?"

He grinned and shook his head. "Not any longer. But I confess, I got into it for a while. It can really suck you in, if you have any interest at all in history."

"So they just all put on uniforms and camp out for the weekend?" She was still trying to take it all in.

"Don't let any of the reenactors hear you say that." Deidre had stopped beside them in time to hear Corrie's words. "It's nothing so simple. They each portray an actual person, and they make sure their gear and uniforms are accurate down to the last little detail. Don't ask Ainsley, or he'll bore you to death over every single battle his infantry unit participated in."

"Come on, Deidre." Lucas's voice was teasing. "I've seen you dressed up in a hoop skirt a time or two."

Deidre shrugged. "If you can't beat them, you have to join them." She spun at the sound of music. "Look, here they come."

The hair on the back of Corrie's neck stood up. Out from the copse of trees, a line of mounted horsemen emerged, moving as slowly as if in a dream. Behind them, gray-clad infantrymen massed, their faces shadowy and indistinct in the cover of the trees. Fifes and drums sent out a call.

"The Bonnie Blue Flag," Lucas murmured. "That's the tune they're playing. Watch. When they get level with the fence line, they're going to charge." His hand closed over hers. "Don't worry. It's perfectly safe."

The horsemen drew nearer, and she spotted Ainsley, his young face set and intent under the brim of his hat. An officer raised his saber, and the sun glinted off the blade. He shouted a command, a bugle blew, and the unit surged forward across the field in a great sweep of men and horses.

The shouts, the gunshots, the Rebel yells nearly deafened Corrie. She took an involuntary step back, and Lucas put his arm around her.

"This is just to entertain the visitors," he said. "You should see it when they do an actual battle. There might be thousands participating."

The advance guard reached the end of the field and planted the colors. Suddenly the charge was over, and men moved toward the tents and the spectators, accepting the cheers and clapping as their due.

"That's exciting enough for me. What else will go on today?"

Lucas seemed to realize he still had his arm around her, and he took a casual step away. "They'll reenact camp life. You can walk around and talk with anyone you like."

"Are you sure my western accent won't get in the way?"

He smiled. "Are you kidding? They'll just be more eager to recruit you. There's a barbecue tent that serves meals. Games for the kids, shooting demonstrations, cannon fire, a little of everything."

"A trip to the past, in other words."

"Just about." His face was shadowed for a moment. "They show you what the War Between the States was like, but they can't really get across the appalling cost in human life."

Before she could pursue the subject, a horse cantered toward them. Ainsley looked down at them. "Well? What did you think of it?"

"That was amazing." Corrie patted the sweaty horse. "You're a time traveler, aren't you?"

Ainsley's face flushed with pleasure. "That's exactly what it's like." He swung down from the saddle. "I'm glad you understand how important it is."

Obviously she'd said the right thing. And with Ainsley smiling at her, she decided not to mention what he'd probably see as Lydia's interference. There was no point in starting another storm.

"Tell me about your uniform and gear. It really looks genuine."

Deidre rolled her eyes. "I refuse to listen to that again. Come on, Lucas. Let's go get some coffee."

By the time Ainsley had described in minute detail every single piece of equipment, and how he'd had to go all the way to Gettysburg to find a sutler who could provide just the right hilt for his saber, Corrie was beginning to understand Deidre's reaction. Like any enthusiast, Ainsley didn't understand why everyone wasn't equally fascinated by his subject.

"Isn't that your friend Patrick over there?" She pointed to the three cannons that were lined up nearby, hoping to divert him from telling her how many dealers he'd contacted before he found the proper buttons.

He shaded his eyes with his hand. "I guess so. We're going to do a demonstration of cannon fire later." He grinned, looking about Jason's age. "We planted a few charges to set off when we fire the cannons. That'll really make it look realistic."

"I can't wait." Actually, Lucas's comment about the number of people who died had dimmed her enthusiasm somewhat, but it would be unkind to let Ainsley guess that.

Ainsley consulted a pocket watch. "It won't be for another hour or so. You might want to get something to eat before then. The food tent's over that way." He pointed to the far side of the tent city.

She spotted Lucas's tall figure standing by the tent. He held a white foam cup in his hand and appeared to be blowing on the contents. For an instant she pictured him in uniform. She already knew how impressive he was on horseback. In uniform—well, maybe it was just as well he'd given up reenacting.

"That sounds like a good idea." For a moment she hesitated, wondering if she should say something to Ainsley about her grandfather. But what could she say that might make a difference? She wasn't in any position to give advice.

"I'll catch you later." His smile was friendly, as if their quarrel had never been. "I'd best give my horse a chance to cool down."

He probably needed to cool down himself in that wool uniform, but it didn't seem to be bothering him. Maybe reenactors got used to the heat. It must have been much worse for the soldiers who'd had to march all day in the heat and then launch themselves into a battle. She watched him cross toward the picket line, and then turned and headed for the food tent.

The field was rutted and pockmarked already from the horses and wagons that had gone over it. She avoided the worst of the ruts, glad she'd worn sneakers. She glanced up, to see Lucas and Deidre standing in front of the food tent, their heads close together, faces serious.

Plotting? She dismissed the idea even as it formed. Lucas wasn't threatened by her, and she'd made some headway with Deidre since the ugly incident with Win. At least with Win out of the picture, she didn't have to look over her shoulder.

He was just supposed to scare you, Deidre had said. Did she admit, even to herself, that Win's tricks could have proved fatal? Well, whether she did or not, Deidre was certainly smart enough not to try anything else.

Lucas glanced up, spotted her, and waved. She waved back, heart ridiculously light. She'd join them, find Eulalie and Jason, have a pleasant day together. It would be a family outing to remember once she'd gone back home.

She took another step, avoiding a raised hummock of grass, her thoughts on family. Was she really starting to think of them that way?

The hummock exploded, dirt and rocks flying. The sound assaulted her, deafened her. The ground came up to meet her, jarring every bone in her body.

"How many fingers do you see?"

Corrie struggled to focus her eyes. Where was she? In a hospital? The vague, fuzzy cloud faded slowly, and a face came into focus—a face with a shaggy white beard and a drooping white mustache. Shrewd gray eyes assessed her from behind wire-rimmed glasses.

"Civil War," she muttered.

"She's delirious," someone said.

The doctor, if that's what he was, laughed. "Down here we call it the War Between the States, but that's the idea."

He stepped back, and Lucas knelt next to her. She realized that what she'd taken for clouds was actually the white canvas roof of a tent. The tent city—the reenactment.

She moved cautiously. "Was I shot?"

Lucas managed a smile, but worry still wrinkled his forehead. "No, sugar, you weren't shot. One of the black powder shells they'd planted to use in the cannon demonstration went off prematurely. You were too close."

"You can take her to the E.R. if you like, but I don't think she's going to have anything worse than bruises and a headache."

Corrie eyed the man's gray uniform with gold piping. "Are you a real doctor or just a reenactor?"

"Both," Lucas said quickly. "Doc Adams is the real thing, don't worry. But maybe I should take you to the hospital."

She moved cautiously, memory returning. Talking to Ainsley, spotting Lucas deep in conversation with Deidre. She felt sore all over, and her head hurt.

"Bruises are starting to feel normal. I'd rather go home."

The doctor gave her an odd look at that, but he nodded. "Take her home and let her rest. If she has any problems other than a headache, take her to the E.R. or give me a call." He patted his pocket, from which protruded an anachronism, a cell phone.

Lucas put his arm around her as she sat up, and she

realized that Eulalie, Deidre and Ainsley crowded the tent doorway.

"Are you sure you're all right?" Eulalie's soft face crinkled, and she looked about to burst into tears. "I'm so sorry this happened. I'd best go along home and take care of you."

Having Eulalie fussing over her didn't sound especially appealing. "You don't need to do that. You've been looking forward to Ainsley's reenactment."

"I'll take her home. Just keep Jason occupied." Lucas's tone didn't leave room for argument. He piloted her to the tent opening. As he passed Ainsley, he paused. "You'd better see if they've found out why that charge went off just when Corrie was walking past."

Ainsley started nervously. "Right. I'll do that."

Outside, the people who had gathered gave her a round of applause, as if she were a football player who'd gotten up after an injury. She waved, trying to smile in spite of the fact that her head was spinning. Someone had moved Lucas's car to the edge of the tents.

"Easy." His arm was strong around her waist as he helped her into the car. She leaned her aching head back against the seat and closed her eyes while he fastened her seat belt and went around the car.

"Are you sure you don't want to go to the hospital?" He started the motor, and the car moved slowly off.

"Don't make me shake my head," she said. "Just take me home."

"All right. Now you're starting to sound like yourself. You had me worried there for a while."

"I was a bit worried myself." She winced as the car hit a rut, and didn't speak again until they'd pulled out onto the road. "Do you think that was an accident?"

For a long moment he didn't answer. Glancing at him, she saw that a deep frown had settled between his brows. At least he wasn't giving her a quick denial.

"Only someone who was familiar with the charges could have set it off that way," he said finally. "It could have just been set incorrectly to begin with. A lot of outfits don't allow those charges. Think they're too dangerous."

"I'll testify to that," she said dryly.

"Just relax. We'll be home in a few minutes."

It was more than a few minutes, of course, traffic being in its usual Saturday snarl. She stopped trying to talk, leaning back and closing her eyes. Now if only she could stop thinking, as well....

Someone who was familiar with the way the charges were set up, Lucas had said. That encompassed quite a few possibilities. Win probably wasn't part of the reenactment, but that didn't mean Deidre didn't have other friends who'd do her a favor. Ainsley certainly knew all about the charges, but would he have mentioned them to her if he'd had something to do with it?

And Lucas himself. She couldn't ignore the fact that he had the knowledge. She might not believe it, but she couldn't ignore it.

By the time they'd reached Baxter's house, her mind had gone around the possibilities so many times that her dizziness was doubled.

She caught Lucas's arm when he'd have led her to her room. "I don't want to go upstairs and have to answer my grandfather's questions right now. I'll rest in the back parlor for a while."

He gave her a concerned look, but led her into the parlor and helped her settle on one of the love seats.

"I'll raid the kitchen and try to get an ice pack without alerting Mrs. Andrews. Is there anything else you want?"

She pressed her hand against her temple. "Aspirin."

He nodded. "Will do. Just relax."

Before she had gone through the events of the day one more fruitless time, he was back. He held the ice bag while she swallowed the aspirin and helped her lean back against the pillows. Then he pulled a chair over and sat down next to her.

She opened one eye to look at him. "I'm fine. You can go now."

"Thanks for the gracious dismissal, sugar, but I think I'll stick around for a while."

He only called her *sugar* when he was annoyed or worried. "Sorry. Thank you for your assistance, but I'm going to rest. I don't require any aid, although it was kind of you to offer."

A smile curved his lips. "Better. Actually, you have every right to be as short as you want to be. It's not my head that's splitting." He covered her hand with his, and his warmth seemed to lessen the pain.

Maybe his presence helped her relax. If so, she couldn't seriously suspect him of setting off that charge, could she?

She let the cold soothe her aching head. Her fingers curved around his almost without conscious intent.

"I know Ainsley was angry over that business with Baxter and the theater." He went on as if there'd been no interruption in their conversation. "But you did tell him about Lydia, didn't you?"

"I never had a chance."

His fingers tightened briefly on hers. "Even so, I find it hard to believe he'd do something to hurt you. This is the kid who would carry a palmetto bug outside rather than swat it."

"That's no doubt why he enjoys running around with a sword in his hand."

"Honestly, Corrie…"

"I know. You don't believe any of them could do anything to me. But these accidents keep happening, don't they?"

"We know about Win." His voice was tight. "Deidre says she didn't know what he was doing. I thought you believed her."

Did she? "I want to," she said slowly. "I'm not sure if it's because I trust her or because I don't like thinking you all hate me."

"I don't hate you." There was so much suppressed emotion in his voice that she turned her head to look at him. He leaned toward her, his face intent. Her breath caught in her throat. She'd never seen his face so open, so filled with everything he felt. "Sometimes I think it would be easier if I did."

The ice bag slid from her head, and she didn't bother to catch it. She touched his cheek tentatively.

"Don't, Lucas. Don't hurt so much."

He covered her hand with his, pressing her palm flat against his cheek, so that the warmth of his skin, the faint roughness of his beard, seemed imprinted on her palm.

"Corrie—" His voice went deep with emotion.

"Shh." She brushed his lips lightly. "You don't have to tell me how wrong this is. I already know. I can't help it."

For an instant she thought he'd bolt from the room. She felt the tension in his muscles. Then he moved, and his lips found hers.

She melted into the kiss, and the world narrowed to the touch of his hand, the warmth of his kiss, the emotion that flooded through her. Longing. Love. She'd never felt so secure, so safe. She'd come home at last.

He drew back slowly. Her lips chilled where his had been. His brown eyes no longer looked topaz. They were so dark they were nearly charcoal.

"I shouldn't have let this happen."

She leaned back, no longer sure what he was feeling. "You weren't the only one involved." When he didn't respond, anger flickered through her. "It shouldn't happen because I don't belong in your world, that's what you mean, isn't it? We've already seen what comes of that with my mother and father."

She wanted him to deny it. To say that they were different, that they didn't have to be trapped by the past.

But he shook his head. He drew her against him, so that her head rested on his shoulder.

"I don't know, Corrie. I don't. I just know I can't walk away."

It wasn't an answer. But it looked as if she'd have to be content with that.

THIRTEEN

"Are you sure you're feeling all right?" Eulalie's face expressed such worry that it almost seemed she felt responsible.

"I'm fine." Corrie was getting tired of saying the words. Those tender moments with Lucas the day before had been interrupted too soon when her grandfather had learned what had happened. He'd actually insisted that his own doctor be summoned to the house, just to be sure Corrie wasn't concussed. She hadn't known quite what to make of his attitude.

And now Eulalie, inviting her over for lunch after church, expressing such concern. She still looked worried, in spite of Corrie's assurances.

"Really." Corrie patted her hand.

"I just feel so responsible," Eulalie said. "I'm the one who insisted we all go to the reenactment. I didn't imagine…"

How would Eulalie have ended that statement, if she hadn't stopped, pink and flustered? Was she thinking, as Corrie did, that it hadn't been an accident?

"It wasn't your fault." She leaned forward, pinning Eulalie's gaze with hers. "But it was someone's."

Eulalie's gaze darted away. "I don't know—it was an accident, that's all. Just an accident."

Did she really believe that? Corrie couldn't tell. If the alternative was to imagine that one of her children had instigated an attack on Corrie, Eulalie would deny it no matter what evidence there was to the contrary.

And there wasn't any evidence, apparently. Lucas had talked at length the previous evening with the event organizers. He seemed convinced they weren't attempting to whitewash anyone, but there was no way of determining what had caused the explosion to go off. So she was left with a load of suspicion and not so much as a handful of proof.

"I have something I want to show you." Eulalie set a thick brown leather album on the lace tablecloth between them. "I know Uncle Baxter showed you some photos of your father, but I thought you might want to see mine, too."

That was the first time Eulalie had actually admitted she was Trey's child. It brought a lump to Corrie's throat.

"Thank you. I'd like see them."

Eulalie flipped through the pages of old photos until she came to the by now familiar smile. "Trey always had that look." Eulalie patted the photo. "So sweet."

"He was a charmer, wasn't he?"

Eulalie nodded. "Not in a manipulative way," she said. "Some men just use charm to get what they want, but not Trey. He really cared about people." A smile softened her lips, and her eyes had a faraway look.

"You loved him," Corrie said, suddenly ashamed. She hadn't even considered that her presence might hurt people who'd loved him.

"He was a brother to me. The best kind of brother—always so sweet and protective." A tear slipped down her cheek. "I've never stopped missing him, you know."

"I didn't realize." Corrie put her hand over Eulalie's,

blinking back tears of her own. "I didn't know how close you were."

"How could you?" Eulalie dashed tears away and sat up a little straighter. "It's ancient history."

"Not to you."

Eulalie seemed to be looking back at that history, and her forehead crinkled. "I was always so terrified when he and Uncle Baxter fought. I was afraid one day he'd go away and I'd never see him again."

"But he did come back."

She nodded. "He came back married." She turned another page, and Corrie saw her mother looking up at her. "Baxter doesn't know I have these. He wouldn't approve."

Corrie leaned over, tracing the image with her fingertip. Gracie and Trey posed against the front door of Trey's house. The next picture showed Trey, laughing, carrying Gracie over the threshold. Then they posed against the stairwell.

Corrie's heart clenched. The stairwell where her father died.

"They looked so happy."

Eulalie nodded, touching her eyes with a lace handkerchief. "They were. So happy, so in love. Baxter was livid, but Trey didn't care."

"What happened to them?" Her fist clenched in frustration. "How could they lose it all so quickly?"

Eulalie shook her head. "Poor Gracie. It didn't take more than a few days for her to realize that she didn't fit in. I don't think Trey ever understood how unhappy that made her. He just thought that marriage should be enough."

A flicker of anger went through her. "People could have tried to help her."

"You mean I could." Eulalie smiled sadly. "I know.

You're right. I just didn't know what to do. I've never been good at standing up to anyone. Uncle Baxter was so angry, and everyone kept saying their marriage couldn't last. I felt caught in the middle. And then when Trey died—" she dabbed her eyes "—Gracie went away, and I thought maybe it was for the best. But when she came back, I hoped we could be friends."

Corrie had been so deep in her own images of Trey and Gracie that she almost missed it. She looked at Eulalie. "When she came back? What do you mean?"

Eulalie looked distressed. "Oh, dear, I shouldn't have said anything. Surely it's better if you don't dwell on such sad old memories."

Corrie gripped her fingers firmly. "I have to know, don't you see? I didn't know my mother came back. Baxter said he didn't see her."

"He didn't. He was away, as I recall. She came to the house, and we talked for a bit. I wish she'd told me about you. I'd like to have known that Trey had a child."

Her head was spinning. So Gracie had done what she'd said. She'd come to Savannah to see Baxter. How then had she ended up in Florida?

"When was that, Eulalie? Do you remember?"

Eulalie shook her head. "Not exactly, no. It was in the summer, I know. In the evening. She came to the house, and I was the only one home."

"But she didn't stay."

"I told her Baxter wasn't expected back until morning, so she said she'd come back the next day, but she didn't. I never saw her again."

"She didn't give you any idea where she was going?" Frustration edged her voice.

"No. I guess I should have asked her to stay here, but I didn't know how Baxter would react. And when she didn't come back—well, I thought she just didn't want to face him."

Corrie leaned back, trying to piece it together. Eulalie assumed Gracie had been afraid of Baxter because that's how she'd feel in that situation. But had Gracie? Surely she hadn't driven halfway across the country only to funk it when the moment came to face her father-in-law.

"I was so sorry," Eulalie said mournfully. "I know I should have done something, but I didn't know what. And then she was gone, and I never had another chance."

She didn't believe it. Corrie crossed the garden slowly, trying to get her mind around everything Eulalie had revealed.

Oh, Eulalie had been telling the truth as far as she saw it. She didn't doubt that. But there had to be something more. It didn't make sense for Gracie to come all that way, even come to the house, and not stay around to see Baxter.

"Corrie, you look far away." Lydia had approached, and she hadn't even noticed until the woman was a few feet away.

"Sorry." She tried to smile. "I guess I was, in a way." Far away, and long ago. "Are you coming or going?" Lydia was dressed in what Corrie mentally classed as her committee meeting wear—navy suit and pearls.

"Returning, thank goodness." Lydia blew out an exasperated breath. "There was an emergency meeting of the church council after service this morning. Honestly, those people can spend more time talking about nothing than anyone I know." She nodded toward her house. "I need a nice tall glass of sweet tea. Come and have one with me."

"That sounds good."

And it was a chance to sound Lydia out about what

Eulalie had told her. She had a lot of respect for Lydia's common sense. That was what undoubtedly made her of such value on all her many committees.

She followed Lydia through the garden door and up to the sunroom that adjoined her kitchen, listening with half an ear to Lydia's tales of the obstructionists who didn't see things her way when it came to doing good works.

Should she blurt out what Eulalie had told her? She hadn't promised to keep it quiet, and Eulalie hadn't asked her to.

"Now, this is nice." Lydia handed her a tall glass, garnished with a wedge of lemon and a sprig of mint, and settled down opposite her on the bright cushions of the wicker love seat. "I haven't talked to you since your accident. I was so worried when I saw you go down."

Corrie blinked, startled. "I didn't realize you were at the reenactment."

"Oh, yes, I wouldn't miss it. I came over when I saw the accident, but by the time I got there, Lucas had carried you into a tent and was shouting for a doctor." She sipped at her tea, eyes bright and interested. "I'm not sure I've ever seen him quite so upset."

She could only hope her expression didn't give anything away. "Everyone was very kind. I was lucky—no aftereffects except a nasty headache."

She made an effort to sip the tea, knowing how sweet it was going to be. She hadn't gotten accustomed to the amount of sugar Savannahians put in their iced tea.

"That doesn't account for the distraction I noticed down in the garden, then."

"No." If she didn't open up to Lydia, she couldn't expect to get anything from the conversation. "I'd been talking to

Eulalie," she said. "She showed me some pictures she had of my mother and father."

"Eulalie kept them?" Her eyebrows arched. "How brave of her. Baxter would have had a fit if he'd known."

"It's none of his business what photographs she has."

"If you think that, my dear, you haven't yet figured out the hold Baxter has on all of them." Lydia leaned back against the floral cushion, dangling a navy pump from her toes as if tired of the heels. No wonder—stockings and heels in this heat. The very idea appalled her.

"Oh, I think I'm getting the message." She sipped at the tea. "At least, now that Eulalie has accepted our relationship, she wanted to show the pictures to me."

Lydia seemed to study her over the rim of her glass. "Did that answer any of your questions?"

Did it? She wasn't sure.

"Baxter said my mother was going to accept money to leave Trey." She hadn't known how much that rankled until it came out. "Do you know anything about that?"

Lydia's gaze fell. "I'm not the right person to ask. After all, I'm not one of your kinfolk."

"That's why I'm asking you." She leaned forward, wishing Lydia would look her in the eye. "You're enough outside the family to give me an honest opinion. I'd appreciate that."

Lydia did look up then, but Corrie couldn't read her expression. "I knew she was going away. She just couldn't handle the situation here." She gave a graceful shrug. "Maybe she thought Trey loved her enough to come after her."

"He didn't, did he?" Bitterness coated her words.

"He couldn't." Lydia's eyes were very dark. "Didn't you realize? That was when he died."

She leaned back as if she'd been shoved. "I—no, I didn't realize." A wave of anger swept through her. "How could I? I'm getting all of it in bits and pieces, whatever anyone decides to tell me at any particular moment. And no one seems to remember the same things."

"That's natural, don't you think? It was a difficult time, and Trey's death knocked every other thought from our minds." Her lips drew in, and for the first time she looked her age. "Gracie stayed for the funeral, and then she left for good."

"Not quite."

Lydia focused a startled look on her. "What do you mean?"

"She came back. When I was six months old, she decided she should tell Baxter about me." Because she wanted money? Corrie wouldn't believe that. "So she came here."

"Are you sure of that?" Lydia's voice was sharp. "Maybe she set out to come here—"

"She arrived. Baxter was out, but she spoke to Eulalie."

"Eulalie." She said the name slowly. "How odd that Eulalie never spoke of seeing her."

"Apparently my mother was supposed to come back the next day, but she never showed up. I imagine Eulalie decided there was no point in stirring up trouble by mentioning it."

Lydia's lips twitched in what might have been meant for a smile. "She was prudent, then. It would have caused trouble."

"I don't understand." Corrie looked down at the glass in her hands. Her fingers ached from gripping it. "She came all this way. It doesn't make sense that she'd go away without seeing Baxter."

"Maybe not to you."

"What do you mean?"

Lydia shrugged. "You're a strong person, Corrie. Probably a lot like that aunt who raised you. You wouldn't back out of a difficult situation. Gracie wasn't like you—she was clinging, always needing someone to prop her up. She might have felt she couldn't face Trey's father."

"That's ridiculous." She had to deny Lydia's assessment, because otherwise she'd have to give up her image of her mother. "She'd have faced anyone for the sake of her child."

Lydia studied her for a moment, as if trying to make up her mind about something. Then she sighed. "I didn't want to say this to you, but I see that I'll have to."

"Say what?" She felt as if she groped through a fog bank. "Just come out with it, whatever it is."

"That night—the night that Trey died." Her face tightened as if the words were painful to her. "That was when Gracie told him that she was leaving. They had a terrible quarrel. I was here, in the house. I heard them up on the stairs, arguing. I heard Trey fall." She sucked in a rasping breath. "I think Gracie pushed him."

Afterward, Corrie was never sure what she said or how she made it out of the house. She certainly couldn't have looked at the staircase.

She found herself in the garden, gasping for breath as if she'd just run five miles. Her heart seemed to be caught in a vise.

This couldn't be true. It couldn't. The garden drowsed in Sunday-afternoon lethargy, but it brought her no peace. She had to talk to someone. She had to talk to Lucas.

He opened the garden door to her knock. She stumbled inside, not sure what she'd have done if he hadn't been home.

"Corrie, what is it?" He grasped her arm, leading her into the large area that was obviously Jason's playroom. He guided her to a well-worn leather couch and sat down beside her, clasping her hands in both of his. "Are you ill? Is it your head?"

"No. Nothing like that." She managed to get her breath and tried to speak calmly. She shouldn't let it affect her this way. She had to make sense, at least, if she was going to tell Lucas about it.

"What then?" His gaze was very intent on her face, so that it was almost a tactile impression. "Who has upset you?"

"Lydia." She took a deep breath. "It's not her fault. I insisted she tell me."

"Tell you what?" His fingers moved in soothing circles on the backs of her hands. "How could Lydia know something that would upset you so much?"

"Because she was there." She closed her eyes against the pain. "She said she was there, in Trey's house, the night he died."

Her father. Trey was her father. The night her father died.

"She was around a lot." He lowered his voice, as comforting as if she were Jason with a cut or a bruise. "In and out of the houses like a member of the family. I suppose she could have been there."

She'd like to be comforted, but it was her heart that was bruised, not her knee.

"She said that Gracie was going to leave." She focused on his face, frowning. "I don't know—maybe that was true. Maybe she was that unhappy."

She read the agreement in his eyes, even though he didn't speak.

She took a deep breath. This was the thing she couldn't

say, but she had to. "Lydia claims she heard the two of them arguing on the staircase. She says she heard Trey fall." Her throat was so tight she could barely force the words out. "She thinks my mother pushed him."

"That's ridiculous." His fingers tightened painfully. "Corrie, you don't believe that, do you?"

"No." She didn't. She couldn't. "But—"

"Don't let yourself think it for a moment. Of course, I was too young then to know, but if there'd been any suspicion of such a thing, there'd have been gossip." His wry smile flickered. "Believe me, there'd have been gossip. I'd have heard something."

"Maybe they hushed it up," she said, longing to be convinced, to believe beyond any shadow of doubt.

"Baxter, hush up a thing like that? Nonsense. If the thought had ever entered his mind, he'd have had the police all over Gracie. He didn't, so it didn't happen."

"But Lydia said it."

"Lydia couldn't have been sure of anything. She doesn't claim to have seen it happen, does she?"

Her numbed brain started working again. Lucas was right. "She didn't say she saw. Just that she heard them quarreling and that she thought Gracie pushed him."

"That's a long way from evidence." He brushed her hair back from her face, his fingertips gentle. "Lydia—I don't know why she'd say something like that. I thought she had better sense."

"Maybe she believed I had a right to know."

"You have a right to know facts. I wouldn't expect Lydia to repeat something so malicious without a shred of proof." He traced the line of her jaw with the backs of his fingers. "Put it right out of your mind, sugar."

"I wish I could." She took a breath. Tell him. Tell him. The words pounded in her skull. "But there's more."

Doubt flickered in his eyes. "What do you mean?"

"Eulalie told me that my mother did come here, six months after I was born. Just about a year after Trey's death. She wanted to see Baxter."

"But Baxter says he didn't see her. Honey, he wouldn't lie about something like that."

"Eulalie said that my mother was supposed to come back and see him. Eulalie never saw her again. But someone here must have." Certainty hardened her voice.

"Why? What makes you think that?"

"Because of what she did." She swallowed, the muscles of her throat working with difficulty. "When she left here, she drove south instead of heading for home. She died in Florida. Drowned."

"I know." He put his arm around her then, pulling her close against him. "You told me."

"I didn't tell you all of it." Even when she closed her eyes, she could see the postcard. "I said we never heard from her again, but that wasn't true. My aunt did. I found it in my aunt's things after she died."

"Found what?"

The steady rise and fall of his chest comforted her. Made it possible to continue with the thing she didn't want to say.

"It was a postcard from Jacksonville. The usual thing—palm trees and sand. On the back, she'd scribbled a few words."

His arm tightened around her, as if in protection. "What did she say?"

"That she couldn't go on. That was all. 'I can't go on.' And her name."

She tried to will the image away, but it wouldn't go. The frivolous front of the postcard juxtaposed tragically against the words.

Lucas rubbed his palm up and down her arm. He wanted to comfort her, but there was no comfort for this.

"You think it was a suicide note."

"Don't you?" She jerked a little away and swung to face him. "What else could it mean? 'I can't go on.' She never intended to come home."

To me. She never intended to come back to me. Wasn't I worth living for?

He seemed to guess some of what she was thinking, because her pain was reflected in his eyes. "Corrie, I'm sorry, so very sorry. But even if she did kill herself, that doesn't mean she didn't love you. She may have been overwhelmed, unable to see past the pain." He hesitated. "The guilt."

"No! She didn't push him. She couldn't have. That goes against everything my aunt ever told me about her. She was gentle, not a fighter. She might have broken down and cried, but she wouldn't have pushed him."

"I know you believe that. But if she did commit suicide—"

"She killed herself because of something that happened when she came back to Savannah." Certainty hardened in her. "Something happened here that made her unable to go on."

"Corrie…" He seemed to marshal his arguments. "Sugar, I know you want to believe that, but you don't have anything to back that up. You said yourself that she didn't see anyone except Eulalie. You can't think Eulalie did anything to drive her to suicide."

"No." The idea was impossible. "Eulalie's too passive to ever make up her mind to do something like that. But

Baxter isn't. If he blamed her for ruining Trey's life, there's no telling what he might do."

"But Eulalie said Gracie didn't see Baxter."

"Eulalie couldn't be sure of that." She shot to her feet. "Only one person knows for sure. Baxter. I'm going to get it out of him."

FOURTEEN

She hadn't, after all, gone to confront Baxter with what she was sure was his lie. Lucas, hand on her arm as if he'd restrain her physically if he had to, had finally convinced her to wait.

Baxter was improving, but he wasn't out of the woods yet. If she upset him, which she was bound to do the way she felt, who knew what would happen? She didn't want to nudge her grandfather into another heart attack, did she?

No, of course not. But she wasn't going to wait forever to get at the truth. Something had sent Gracie off course, had led her to Florida and a watery grave. She meant to find out what.

Eventually they'd come to a compromise of sorts. She'd wait a few days and talk to the doctor before she confronted Baxter.

So, trying to keep herself occupied in the meantime, she'd come out to Lucas's farm to take him up on the invitation to go riding. Mr. Davis had saddled up the mare she'd ridden the last time, and he'd finally let her go with elaborate directions and cautions.

He hadn't needed to be so cautious. She'd follow the same trail she'd taken with Lucas and Jason that other time—she remembered it well enough. She had no intention of wandering off and getting lost. And she was certainly safer here than in the city.

She patted the mare's neck, bending as they went under the low-lying branches of a live oak. In spite of the heat of the day and the clouds of gnats that rose from the grass, she felt a surge of pure pleasure. How could Lucas bear to spend virtually all his time in a city when he had a place like this to escape to?

The answer to that was unfortunately too clear. He didn't spend time at the farm because he didn't want to make the situation difficult for his son. If Jason couldn't ride, he'd forgo the pleasure for himself, too.

The stream came into view ahead of them, and the mare quickened her pace. Corrie let her move into a jog trot, taking the jolting with the ease of long practice.

Was Lucas right about Jason? She frowned. Certainly the boy's asthma attack had been frightening, but it hadn't occurred until they were currying the horses at the very end of their ride. Maybe Jason would be able to cope with riding if someone else did the currying. That was probably when the dander flew the most.

And then there was the emotional factor. She hadn't forgotten, even if Lucas had, that they'd been quarreling when Jason became short of breath.

She hadn't said that to Lucas. She hadn't wanted to give him anything else to feel guilty about. But still, she wondered. It was a harsh penalty, not to be able to do the thing you wanted most in the world. If she were Jason's parent…

But she wasn't. Lucas, even when he comforted her in his arms, even when he kissed her, had never hinted at anything like that.

They reached the stream. Corrie slid from the mare's back and let her drink. She settled on a large flat stone at the edge of the water, holding the reins loosely in her hand.

Lucas wouldn't suggest anything closer between them. She knew that now. He, like everyone else, had seen what Trey and Gracie had done to each other. He wouldn't run the risk of that.

And even if he accepted the fact that this was a different era, that they weren't as young and naive as Trey and Gracie had been, she suspected he carried too many scars from his marriage to be ready for another relationship.

It was just as well, even though her heart ached when she thought of it. She wouldn't make the same mistake her mother had made. She didn't belong here, and she had sense enough to know it.

The mare whickered softly, flicking her tail to chase away the horseflies. Her ears flicked forward, then back. The stream chuckled and burbled over the rocks, and a faint breeze cooled Corrie's overheated face.

There were things she'd miss about this place, and this was one of them. She scooped up a handful of small pebbles from the creek bank and let them slip through her fingers. Once she'd spoken to Baxter, maybe she'd be able to accept that she'd learned all she could. She'd head for home.

Something rustled in the thick underbrush across the creek. The mare lifted her head again, blowing softly.

"It's okay, sweetheart. Just a rabbit, probably."

The horse moved restlessly, not assured by her words. Her hooves clattered against the rocks underfoot.

"It's okay," she said again. If she sat here any longer, she'd doze off. She shoved herself to her feet. "We'll just—"

A sharp crack broke the air, and shards flared from the rock where she'd sat an instant ago.

The mare reared, threatening to bolt. If she hadn't been grasping the reins, she'd have lost the animal for sure. If Belle had come back without her—

A second shot struck the earth in front of her. This wasn't a random hunter, shooting carelessly at rabbits and missing. This was someone after her.

Adrenaline pumped through her veins. Get out. She had to get out.

She grasped the pommel of the saddle, ready to pull herself up. But wait—maybe the shooter had failed because the horse was sheltering her.

"Okay, baby." She shortened the reins. "We're going to go. Take it easy."

In a swift, clear movement she swung onto the horse's back, immediately ducking down on the side away from the shooter. Her heart pounded. At least this time, he'd made the mistake of picking a place where she was in her element. She could do this.

She nudged the horse, hanging low on the animal's side. Belle whinnied, tossing her head uneasily. Branches snapped and rustled. The shooter was attempting to move into a better position.

Now or never. As soon as Belle's feet had gained the solid surface of the trail, she slapped the reins. Belle sprang forward, Corrie hanging on to her side for dear life.

They thundered down the trail, with Corrie's heart beating as fast as the horse's. Another shot rang out, clipping a tree branch a few feet ahead.

"Come on, Belle." Leaning on the horse's neck, Corrie urged her on. A few more feet, and they'd be around the bend in the path. The shooter wouldn't follow, would he? He must know that Mr. Davis would be waiting back at the stable for her.

A bullet whistled over her head, burying itself in a tree trunk. Evidence, she thought, but she wouldn't be hanging around long enough to collect it. She had to get to the barn, had to get back to Lucas.

She didn't pause to assess the reasons why getting back to Lucas was the only way she'd feel safe. She dug her heels in and sent Belle cannoning down the trail that led to the barn.

Lucas discovered he was glancing at his watch yet again and looked away, frustrated. Corrie would get back from the farm when she got back. He ought to be concentrating on these figures, not acting like a lovesick idiot.

Love. He didn't want to use that word in connection with his feelings for Corrie. It was too dangerous. He'd failed so miserably with his wife—how could he take the chance of doing that again?

Besides, there was Jason to consider. And the family's attitude. To say nothing of the differences that had doomed Trey and Gracie's relationship. How could he expect Corrie to face all that?

He'd been staring at the same screen for the past twenty minutes. Sighing, he swung the chair away from it and walked to the window of Baxter's study, looking down at the garden.

He should be relieved that Corrie had decided to take him up on the offer to go riding at the farm. She'd be safe there, and at least she wasn't here, wanting to confront Baxter with her questions.

He rubbed the back of his neck, where tension had taken

up permanent residence in recent weeks. Her mother's suicide was a terrible burden for Corrie to handle. She had a
right to know anything that might shed light on it. On the
other hand, finding out could just be opening her to more
hurt. Or hurting other people.

He took a deep breath. Once he'd known where to take
problems and decisions. Somehow, after Julia's death, his
guilt had closed off that line of communication.

Father? The word was tentative. *I know You haven't
moved away from me. I'm the one who left. Maybe I've gone
too far away. I don't know. I just know I can't make these decisions on my own. I need help. Show me the right path.*

A figure moved in the garden below, drawing his attention. It was Corrie, back from her ride. His attention sharp-
ened. She was hurrying toward the house, and her
face—something was wrong, very wrong.

He thundered down the stairs, reaching the garden door
just as she came in. He reached for her. Catching a shaky
breath, she darted into his arms.

He wrapped his arms around her, feeling the tremors she
was trying to suppress. He pressed his lips against her
shining hair.

"What is it? Tell me, Corrie. What happened?"

She caught a little choking breath and raised her face
toward his. "I guess riding wasn't such a good idea after
all. Someone shot at me."

"Shot at you?" He echoed her words, fear and doubt bat-
tling for control. "Are you sure? I mean—"

"I know a rifle shot when I hear one." A flash of anger
crossed her face like lightning. "I was down near the stream.
The shooter hit the rock where I'd been sitting. If it hadn't
been for Belle—" The shudder went through her again.

"She didn't bolt?" Surely, if someone had been shooting that close, even a well-trained animal like Belle would have taken off.

"She tried." Corrie's smile flickered. "I wasn't letting her leave without me. I managed to keep her between me and the shooter until we got out of range."

She leaned back, letting go of him. "Sorry." She pushed her hair back from her face, her hand still trembling a little in spite of the brave front she was attempting. "I didn't mean to throw myself at you."

"You can do that any time." He tucked the hair behind her ear. "I'm just thankful you're all right. I never should have let you go out there alone."

Her brows lifted. "Let? Nobody lets me do anything. I'm a big girl."

"Right. Sorry." He took a breath, trying to force down his anxiety enough to think this through. "There was some talk of illegal hunters trespassing on the property."

She gave him a level, challenging look. "Is that what you want to believe?"

That nettled him. "It's not a question of what I want. It's a question of what we tell the police."

"The police?" Her blue eyes widened.

"Of course the police." It made him angry that she could even imagine he wouldn't take this seriously. "Whether it was accidental or deliberate, the police have to investigate. The question is, do we tell them the whole story? What did you tell Ephraim Davis?"

"I told him about the shots. He assumed it was a hunter."

He nodded. That was logical, but Ephraim didn't know the whole story. "And the police?"

He waited. This was up to Corrie, in the end. She was

right—she was a grown woman and she made her own decisions.

She turned away, frowning at the arrangement of roses on the table, but he didn't think she saw it. He wouldn't push.

Finally she turned back to him. "Everything that's happened could have been an accident except what we know Win did. I think we have to tell the police about him."

He nodded, lifting the receiver from the phone that stood on the table.

She caught his hand, staying the movement. "Aren't you going to try and talk me out of it? Point out that it will make things difficult for Deidre? Upset Baxter?"

"No."

Her eyebrows lifted. "Just no?"

He smiled. "Just no. Do you think I'd risk a hair on your head for the sake of sparing us embarrassment?"

That came out a little more heated than he'd intended. He was letting his feelings show, even though he didn't see any future for those feelings.

Corrie looked at him for a long moment, and he thought he read in her eyes the same caring mixed with caution that must be written in his own.

They cared. They didn't know what to do with that caring.

The only thing he could do was take the next step. He lifted the phone and called the police.

Talking with the police proved to be less intimidating than Corrie might have expected. They were polite, almost excessively so, either from native Southern etiquette or out of awe of the Manning name. Finally it was done, and they were gone.

Lucas looked at her with raised brows. "Not so bad, was it?"

"No." She moved her shoulders uneasily. "I just hope they're not going to hassle Deidre too much."

"They have to ask." He frowned. "I don't know how Win would have known you were there, unless he's been following you, but it seems like the kind of thing he might have done. He blames you for breaking up his relationship with Deidre."

"If I did, I can't be sorry for that." The uneasiness moved through her again. Convenient, to have a nice handy outsider to blame. Either Win, or the supposed illegal hunters, would be a relief to Lucas, at a safe remove from the family.

"At least Baxter didn't find out about it." Lucas glanced up the stairwell, as if afraid he'd see the elderly man attempting to come down. "I warned everyone not to tell him."

"Do you think that will work? From what I've seen, he has his own ways of knowing what's going on with everyone."

"Not this time," Lucas said, with more assurance than he probably felt. He came back toward her, concern warming his eyes. "You must be exhausted."

"I feel like I've been on a three-day trail ride in a storm." She managed a smile. "But there's really nothing wrong with me. If our shooter had better aim…"

He sank down on the couch next to her, frowning a little. "That's one way of looking at it."

It took her a moment to catch up. "You mean he might have meant to frighten me, not kill me."

"It's a possibility."

She nodded slowly. "I guess. I'd have to say it doesn't bring me much comfort." She met his eyes. "Do you think I ought to leave?"

His hand closed over hers, and she felt the familiar flood of warmth it engendered. "I want you to be safe, Corrie."

He wouldn't ask her to stay. The knowledge settled deep within her. Whatever they'd shared, whatever feelings they had, he wouldn't ask her to stay.

She took a steadying breath. "I won't leave until I've talked to Baxter. I can't. I can't go back with questions unanswered and spend the rest of my life wondering."

"I understand." His fingers moved slowly on the back of her hand. "But what you're asking—"

A knock at the door cut off the rest of that thought, but she knew what it was. He believed she'd never really know what had driven her mother to suicide.

She watched him move with that long-limbed grace to the door. It would hurt to leave without knowing. But leaving would be painful even if all her questions were answered, because leaving meant she'd never see Lucas again.

Ainsley erupted into the room, his thin face flushed. "I saw the police. What's going on?" He looked from her to Lucas. "Tell me."

He sounded a little overurgent, even for him. Lucas looked at him with eyebrows raised.

"There's been an attack on Corrie. What do you know about it?"

Ainsley's flush deepened. "That was just an accident at the reenactment. Why would you want to call the police?"

"I'm not talking about the reenactment. Corrie went riding out at my place this afternoon. Someone with a rifle took a few shots at her."

Ainsley was suddenly as pale as he'd been flushed. He crossed to her, dropping on one knee to clasp her hands urgently. "Were you hurt?"

"No." She freed her hands gently. "But I'm getting a bit weary of near misses. If you know something, Ainsley, now is that time to say so."

His face set in that sulky look. "I don't know why you're asking me."

"She's asking you because you know something," Lucas said. "I may not be able to prove it, but I'm convinced that shell didn't go off by accident just when Corrie was walking by. And it certainly wasn't an accident that someone shot at her."

Something close to panic showed in Ainsley's face. "You can't mean me. You can't think that I—"

Lucas frowned, the lines in his face deepening as he looked at the boy he must think of as a younger brother. "I don't want to believe it. But someone very familiar with the reenactment set that charge off. And someone followed Corrie to the farm today." His jaw tightened. "You weren't at the office this afternoon, Ainsley. Where were you?"

Ainsley sprang to his feet. "You can't believe that of me! Lucas, you know me. You know I couldn't hurt anyone."

"I know you enough to know when you're hiding something, Ainsley. Tell me, or I'll tell the police."

Lucas wouldn't, she felt sure. He hadn't mentioned Ainsley to the police, and he hadn't even told her that Ainsley had been missing from work. But if Ainsley thought he would...

Indecision clouded Ainsley's eyes and made his lips tremble. He flung himself away several steps, and then turned to face Lucas.

Lucas waited, and her heart hurt at what this must be costing him. He must feel as if he sided with her against his family.

"All right!" Ainsley flung out his hands. "I—it wasn't me. It was Pat." He swung toward Corrie. "You remember my friend. He didn't mean to hurt you." His flush deepened. "I'd been shooting off my mouth I guess, talking about how you'd given me away to the old man. When he saw you walking toward the buried shell, he thought he'd set it off, just to scare you. He didn't realize how long the time delay was, and you were a lot closer than he thought you'd be. I can tell you, it scared the—it scared him half to death."

"And this afternoon?" Lucas looked grim. "Did that scare him, too?"

"No, he didn't! You have to believe me. He wouldn't do that. We were together at the theater this afternoon." He shot Lucas a defiant look. "You know perfectly well I'm not doing anything useful at the company. I may as well skip out early."

Lucas would probably like to agree with that assessment, but he couldn't. "You're being paid a salary to be there. You can't skip out any time you like. As for this afternoon—"

"Pat and I were at the theater all afternoon," he said, an edge of desperation in his voice. "You can check if you want to—the whole cast was there." He turned to Corrie. "Please, Corrie. I wouldn't do anything to hurt you, even if you did tell Uncle Baxter."

She opened her mouth to deny it, but Lucas beat her to it.

"Corrie didn't tell Baxter. Lydia did. She apparently ran across some mention of your theater in one of those endless arts committees she's on."

Ainsley's face bore an almost comical look of consternation. "Lydia! I never thought of her. Corrie, I'm sorry."

She thought, not for the first time, that Lydia was a bit

too involved in family matters. "It's all right, Ainsley. If I'd told you as soon as I knew…" She let that trail off. Even if he hadn't know the truth, the whole business didn't reflect well on Ainsley or his friend.

He ducked his head, as if embarrassed, and gave her that shy smile. He looked at Lucas. "I'll write off those names for you. And I'll be at the office early tomorrow. I promise. Please don't turn Pat in. He didn't intend to hurt anyone."

"That's up to Corrie," Lucas said.

She could only hope Patrick was as upset as Ainsley claimed. "I guess we don't need to tell them—they're not investigating that."

"Thanks, thanks." Ainsley rushed out, shutting the door as if afraid she would change her mind.

She rose, smiling. "At least Ainsley managed to solve one of our mysteries. And to rule himself and Patrick out of today's events."

"I'll follow up on his alibi," Lucas said, taking her hands in his. "At this point I'm not taking anything for granted."

"Maybe you ought to check up on my story, too," she suggested. "I could show you the tree with the bullet."

"I trust you, Corrie." He smiled a little wryly. "Things have changed in a few short weeks, haven't they?"

She nodded, not sure he knew how much they'd changed, at least for her. "I think I'll say good-night. Being shot at seems rather tiring."

His hands tightened, and for a moment she thought he'd pull her into his arms. Then he bent and kissed her cheek, his lips warm on her skin. "Good night, sugar. Sleep well."

She went out quickly, before she could give away just how much his kiss meant to her.

Corrie hadn't thought she'd sleep, but she fell almost

immediately into a deep, dreamless sleep. It must have been the middle of the night when she woke with the realization that Lucas had been wrong about one thing. He hadn't succeeded in keeping it from Baxter.

Her grandfather stood next to her bed, staring down at her. While she lay in startled immobility, he patted her cheek gently. Then he turned and made his way slowly out of the room.

FIFTEEN

The house felt even quieter than usual the next day. Corrie moved restlessly from her room to the garden and back again, unable to settle to anything. Lucas had stopped by while she was having breakfast, looking distracted, and asked her not to go anywhere alone. She'd have argued, but she thought he was right.

The weather, seeming to catch her mood, treated her to lowering skies and humidity so thick you could cut it with a knife. After her visit to the garden began to feel more like a trip to a sauna, she was only too glad to retreat into the house again.

She was mounting the stairs slowly when she encountered Deidre coming down. She hesitated, wary, not sure what to expect. She and Deidre had begun to form a cautious relationship in recent days, but telling the police about Win might have changed that.

The expression Deidre turned on her didn't encourage her to expect any friendly comments. "You've outdone yourself this time, haven't you, Cousin?" She made the title sound like an epithet.

Corrie stiffened. "If this is about Win—"

"Win? Why should I care about Win?" Deidre seemed

to toss her old boyfriend away as if he'd never been part of her life.

If she wasn't upset about the possibility of the police questioning Win about the shooting, Corrie couldn't imagine what had her in a snit now.

"Just tell me what this is about, Deidre. I'm too tired to play guessing games."

"As if you didn't know." Her eyes flashed dangerously, her thin hand grasping the railing as if she'd like to tear it loose and hit Corrie with it.

Corrie sighed. "Skip the dramatics. I really don't know what you're talking about."

"Baxter." She threw the name at her. "I'm talking about Baxter. As if you didn't know, he's sent for his attorney. Three guesses as to what he wants to see him about. Congratulations, Cousin. You're probably going to scoop the lot and leave the rest of us out in the cold."

"That's ridiculous." She stared at Deidre, shocked that she actually appeared serious. "He wouldn't do that. I don't want him to."

Deidre's smile twisted. "Tell that to someone who might believe it. I don't."

She resisted the urge to give Deidre a good shake. "I'll do better than that. I'll see my grandfather and put an end to this."

Leaving Deidre staring after her, she ran up the steps and headed straight for Baxter's bedroom.

Of course it wasn't that easy. She had to run the gamut of nurses first, but finally she was admitted to the room. Lucas was there, seated across from Baxter at the small round table, papers between them.

Baxter raised his eyebrows at her rapid entrance. "So

tempestuous, Corrie. Is this visit really necessary? Lucas and I have a lot of work to get through."

"I think it is." She came to a halt at the table.

Lucas swept papers together. "I'll leave you alone."

"You don't need to do that," Corrie said. "I don't mind you hearing what I have to say."

Baxter waved him back to his seat. "Stay. I don't have any secrets from you." He looked at Corrie. "Well, Corrie?"

She put her palms on the table, leaning toward him. "Deidre just told me you've sent for your attorney."

He looked annoyed. "I don't know what business that is of Deidre's. Or yours, for that matter."

It wasn't, of course, if he wanted to see his lawyer on any other matter. She took a breath, trying to still her racing pulse.

"She's made an assumption that you've sent for him in order to put me in your will. I want you to tell her she's wrong."

"Why would I do that? She's not wrong, although she is impertinent. That's exactly what I plan to do."

"You can't."

His face froze. "On the contrary, I can do whatever I like with what is mine." His words dropped out like icicles.

"I don't want anything from you."

Except the truth, and she was unlikely to get that. If she asked him straight out, right now, about Gracie's visit, would he even admit seeing her?

"It's only right, Corrie." Lucas was using that calm, reasoning tone he kept for the rest of the family. "You're Trey's child, and naturally your grandfather wants to change his will to reflect that."

"I don't want anything. He didn't do anything for my mother when she was alive. It's too late now."

Baxter's face darkened alarmingly. "I'm not trying to make amends. I will do what I want with what is mine, and if I chose to leave something to you, I will."

"I won't accept."

"I don't care if you give it to a home for cats—"

"Calm down, both of you." Lucas's voice had an unexpected edge that had both of them turning to look at him. "You're behaving like children."

The severity of his frown made her ashamed. Her grandfather was ill, and she was shouting at him. "I'm sorry. I shouldn't upset him, but—"

Lucas cut her words short with a gesture. He transferred his frown to her grandfather. "You're as bad as she is, Baxter. It must be an inherited trait. Don't argue—just tell Corrie what you have in mind."

For a moment she thought Baxter would flare out at him. Then he leaned back in his chair, fatigue carving deeper lines in his face.

"Trey's property should have gone to his wife when he died, but it was still in my name."

He hesitated for a moment, and she thought he was finished. She moved slightly, but before she could speak, he shook his head.

"I should have traced her—found out what happened to her. I didn't, and you suffered because of that."

She didn't know what to say. This penitent mood was totally unlike anything she'd seen from Baxter in the past.

Lord, I thought knowing who my parents were would resolve all my questions, but it hasn't. It's opened up a new field of questions, doubts, responsibilities. Help me to do the right thing now.

"I appreciate your saying that," she said slowly. Was that

what he'd been thinking about in the middle of the night, when he'd stood at her bedside? "To be honest, I have no complaints. My great-aunt loved me and did her best for me. I'm not sure any child needs more than that."

"That doesn't change what I do," Baxter said, with the return of a little of his former arrogance. "I'm sure your aunt was a good woman, but you should have received what was Trey's."

"I don't want—"

He glared at her, but some of the energy faded from his face, as if the conversation had pushed him beyond his limits.

"I intend to sign over to you what had been Trey's. His house, the value of some other property that had been promised to him. Don't argue."

Perhaps she continued to look stubborn, because Lucas interceded, leaning toward her. "It's only right, Corrie. What was your father's property comes to you. Right ethically, right legally. You wouldn't ask Baxter to break the law by keeping it now that he knows of your existence, would you?"

Put that way, she didn't know how to respond. "I guess not."

"Good." His smile sent a wave of caring through her. "That's settled, then."

"Not quite." Baxter's voice rasped. "My will. When is that lawyer coming?"

"After you've rested." Lucas nodded to the nurse, who'd been hovering in the background, and she came toward the table.

"Maybe I can ask…" Corrie began, a little desperately. She hadn't come here for an inheritance, but she'd give a lot to ask him about her mother's last visit.

Baxter frowned, as if to quarrel, but Lucas got up and

took her arm. "Later," he murmured. "He's had all he can handle now. Let him rest."

Again, he'd left her without a choice. She nodded, still reluctant, and left the room.

The house was still too quiet. She had to find something to occupy herself until she could talk to Baxter again. Now there were two things weighing on her that couldn't be addressed until he was well enough to deal with them—her mother's last visit and the question of his will.

She found herself smiling wryly. If she'd ever imagined that rich people had it made, she'd learned her lesson. Money seemed to bring more problems than it caused.

She wandered out into the garden, hoping she wouldn't meet any of the family there. She didn't want to deal with Ainsley's protestations of innocence or Deidre's fiery anger.

Deidre needed something worthwhile to do with her life, so that she could expend all that passion on a career she loved. Baxter's attitude, as well as her mother's, kept her a prisoner. Having money, or having the promise of money, hadn't brought happiness to either Ainsley or Deidre.

Forgive me for the times I've envied people I thought had it easy, Father. I judged them without walking in their shoes. I hope I'll know better in the future.

She was still at loose ends, but she felt better, clearer, somehow. She got up, stretching. Maybe Mrs. Andrews would let her into the kitchen. She could teach the woman how to make chili.

The housekeeper wasn't interested in chili, but Corrie spent a soothing couple of hours making pies. Jason wandered in, apparently at loose ends, as well, and Mrs. Andrews provided an extra rolling pin so that he could join the fun.

That might well have been the most pleasant afternoon she'd spent in that house. She was vaguely aware of people coming and going up the front stairs, but she shut her mind to the possibility of lawyers and wills. By the time Eulalie collected Jason, clucking over the amount of flour on his person, she felt soothed, calm, and ready to face whatever came next.

She took her time over showering and dressing for dinner, wondering why she was bothering but enjoying it, nonetheless. At home, she'd have popped a bowl of chili in the microwave and eaten at the kitchen table in jeans.

Here, even if she dined alone, the housekeeper would insist on serving her in solitary splendor. At least she'd persuaded the woman to let her eat in the sunny breakfast room instead of at the vast table in the dining room.

She came out, closing the bedroom door, and hesitated for a moment on the landing. Should she try to see her grandfather again? Maybe, if he'd accomplished what he'd set out to do with the lawyers, he'd be in a satisfied mood and ready to talk.

She crossed to the bedroom door and rapped gently. No answer. Maybe the nurse hadn't heard her. She tapped a little louder.

Nothing.

She frowned at the door. One of the nurses was supposed to be with Baxter at all times. What was going on?

She grasped the knob, turning it gently, and eased the door open, ready to retreat at a glare from the nurse. She peered around the door's edge.

The curtains were drawn across the wide windows, plunging the space into gloom. Baxter must be sleeping, then. She could hear the rasp of his breath.

She drew the door toward her and then stopped, her mind registering what she'd seen. The nurse who was on duty was the placid, round one who always sat with her knitting in the most comfortable chair. The knitting lay in a colorful heap on the seat of the chair, but the nurse was nowhere to be seen.

The door whispered across the carpet as she pushed it open. Of course the woman had the right to a break now and then, but Corrie couldn't shake the apprehension that grasped the back of her neck. Maybe she should stay until the woman came back. It seemed wrong for Baxter to lie, defenseless in sleep, alone.

She crossed toward the bed, careful to walk softly. She didn't want to wake him. Just to be sure—

Sure what? She struggled to recognize the source of her apprehension. Baxter was fine, he was sleeping.

Then, as she got closer, she knew what it was. Those deep, rasping breaths reminded her, too vividly, of sitting with her aunt the night she died.

Her rational mind said there was no connection, but emotion sent her surging to the bed. Baxter's hand lay lax on the gray counterpane. She clasped it in hers, appalled at how cold he felt.

"Grandfather!" She hadn't called him that before, but the word burst out. "Are you all right? Wake up!"

He didn't move. There wasn't the faintest flicker of response to her raised voice.

Panic ripped through her. She seized him by the shoulders, attempting to rouse him. "Baxter, wake up."

"What are you doing?" The nurse stood just inside the door, holding a tray with a steaming cup on it.

"There's something wrong with him." Relief swept

through her. The woman would know what to do. "He won't wake up."

The nurse shoved the tray onto the nearest table and pushed past Corrie to put one hand on her patient's pulse and lift his eyelid with the other. A second later she turned an accusing face to Corrie.

"He can't wake up," she snapped. "What did you do to him?"

Corrie waited in the back parlor for the doctor to come down. Lucas had stayed upstairs with him, and the rest of the family, including Lydia, who seemed to consider herself one of them, had gathered here.

Corrie sat alone on one of the love seats. The others were grouped together opposite her, and the nurse's words still seemed to ring in the air. *What did you do to him?*

She wrapped her arms around herself, as if for protection from all those inimical stares.

Please, Lord. What they think of me doesn't matter. Just please be with my grandfather. Hold him in Your hands and give him strength. Please.

"He saw his lawyer this morning," Deidre began, as if unable to keep silent any longer.

"We won't talk about that now," Eulalie said, eyes red-rimmed from weeping.

"Really, Mama—"

"Drop it, Deidre." Lydia's voice was crisp. "It's both inappropriate and in poor taste."

Deidre muttered something, but she subsided.

Corrie took a deep breath and tried to ease the tension that gripped her. Lydia's cool common sense was an asset at the moment.

Minutes ticked past, measured by the ornate grandfather clock against the far wall. Finally steps sounded on the stairs. Everyone in the room seemed to stiffen, heads turning toward the archway.

The doctor entered, closely followed by Lucas.

Eulalie started to her feet. "Is he—how is he?"

"He'll do, I think." The lines in the doctor's face had deepened. "Anyone with less determination would probably be gone by now."

"What happened to him?" Deidre's question flew at him like an arrow.

An expression of professional reticence crossed his face. "He seems to have had an overdose of medication. It's unclear how that happened."

"Unclear?" Deidre's voice was shrill. "How can you say that? We all heard what the nurse said. She found Corrie bending over him."

"He was already unconscious then." Lucas spoke for the first time. "Clearly the overdose, if that's what it was, had happened already."

He was defending her, in a way. But he also wasn't looking at her. Corrie's heart seemed to shrivel. If Lucas thought her capable of attempted murder, even the possibility of friendship between them was gone.

"Is that right, Doctor?" Lydia's cool question didn't indicate any bias one way or the other. But if Lydia thought Corrie's mother guilty of murder, she was hardly likely to defend her.

"I don't care to speculate." He obviously didn't like to be put on the spot.

"Are you calling the police?" she continued.

"Certainly not." His mouth set in a firm line. "That's the only thing I'm sure about. Baxter wouldn't want that."

He was undoubtedly right, but Corrie couldn't feel that was the answer. "How are you going to protect him, then?"

He gave her a cautious look, not as hostile as those she'd gotten from the family, but not exactly friendly, either. "I'm putting on new nurses, people I can count on to keep everyone out." He glanced at Lucas. "Lucas and I are agreed on that. No one goes in to see Baxter until he wakes up and tells us what happened, if he can."

"What do you mean, if he can?" She couldn't sit any longer. She surged off the love seat and crossed the space between them. "You said he was going to be all right."

"I think he won't suffer any permanent damage, but that doesn't mean he'll remember what happened. He may not even know."

Deidre stood. "Who are we kidding? We all know what happened here."

"Deidre—" Eulalie tugged at her arm without success.

"Uncle Baxter changed his will. He made her his heir. And she tried to kill him before he could come to his senses and change it back again."

She'd known that was what they were thinking, but it was far worse to hear it out loud. She looked at Lucas. His was the only opinion she cared about. But he wasn't looking at her. He was frowning at Deidre.

"That's completely out of line, Deidre. There's nothing to be gained by making random accusations. Hopefully Baxter will regain consciousness soon, and we'll know what happened. In the meantime, I'd suggest you all clear out. I'll call you if there's any change."

For a moment she thought Deidre would strike him, the fury in her eyes was so intense.

"You! Who made you boss, I'd like to know. You're not Baxter's blood kin."

"No," he said softly. "Corrie is Baxter's closest blood kin. Would you like her to take over?"

Deidre recoiled. "That's ridiculous. You can't—she can't—"

Lydia took her arm in a firm grip. "Enough, Deidre. Your mother is exhausted and upset. Help me take her home. You can't do anything here."

Ainsley got to his feet and helped his mother up. "She's right, Dee. Let's go. We can trust Lucas to take care of our interests."

Of course they could. Her heart cramped. She could have predicted this. It didn't really matter to them that she was Trey's daughter. She was still the outsider, and that's what she'd always be.

Tears blinded her eyes suddenly, and she knew she had to get out before they could see her cry.

"Corrie," Lucas began.

She shook her head and darted past him toward the stairs and the safety of her room.

She'd wept. She'd prayed. Finally, feeling emotionally drained, she sank down in the chair next to the window and reached for her Bible.

The pages fell open to the familiar Psalm. She'd begun to read the reassuring words when she realized something was missing. The photo of her mother and father that she always kept at that spot—it wasn't there.

She moved her hand over the page. This couldn't be.

She always kept the photo at that verse. She flipped through the pages, forward and backward. She found the bookmark she'd made in Bible School in the fourth grade and the memorial card from her aunt's funeral. Nothing else. The photograph was gone.

She dropped to her knees, running her hand across the carpet, lifting the dust ruffle to check under the bed. Finally she sat back on her heels.

Ridiculous, to let this get to her after everything else that had happened, but suddenly the tears were rolling down her face again. Someone had been in her room. Someone had taken it.

She pushed herself to her feet, wiping the tears away impatiently. Someone. Someone who hated her, someone who would try to kill an ailing, elderly man—that someone had free access to the house.

Her blood chilled. To her grandfather. The doctor might say he had full confidence in the nurses he'd sent in. He'd thought that about the previous one, and she'd wandered off to fix herself a cup of tea and left Baxter alone for who knew how long.

He was her grandfather. Lucas probably hadn't meant it this way, but he was right. She was his nearest blood kin. It was up to her to see that he was safe.

SIXTEEN

Silence muffled Baxter's house, and Lucas began to feel as if his head were muffled, as well—as if he couldn't hear the sounds around him. He'd been sitting in the chair he'd pulled up to the study door for what seemed like hours, his gaze glued to the crack he'd left in the door.

No one could approach the hall door without his seeing him or her, and no one could come through the study without his being aware of it. Baxter was safe while he was on guard.

No one would try, in all likelihood. Certainly all of them realized he'd be here throughout the night.

Still, he'd never have expected that someone would make an outright attack on Baxter. All of the venom or jealousy or whatever it was had so far been directed at Corrie.

Corrie. By shifting his position slightly he could see the door to her room. She'd held up under all the pressure so far, and he had to admire her courage. In his heart, he was convinced she couldn't have done anything to Baxter, but his head urged caution. After all, how could he believe that of any of them—people he'd loved and trusted for years?

Hang on, that was all he could do. Protect Baxter and

hope that when he awoke, he'd know who had done this thing. Then, no matter what the difficulty, they'd find a way to handle it.

He blinked, wishing he'd thought to ask the house-keeper to bring up a fresh pot of coffee before she went to bed. Rolling his head from side to side, he tried to ease the tightness from his neck. Nothing would happen, he told himself again, but still, he'd stay on duty.

A soft click echoed in the stillness. He leaned forward again, just in time to see Corrie's door open. Corrie stepped into the hallway, stood for a moment as if listening for any sound, and then walked toward her grandfather's bedroom door.

Something seemed to freeze inside him. He rose silently, waiting. When she reached for the knob of the bedroom door, he swung the study door open. She whirled to face him, eyes wide.

"Lucas." She kept her voice soft. "I thought you'd be here someplace. How is he?"

Give her the benefit of the doubt. She hadn't done anything wrong.

"There's been no change in his condition." The words sounded stilted to his ears, and he tried to soften them. "Get some sleep, Corrie."

She shook her head in instant negation. "I couldn't. Not when I know…" She stopped.

"Know what? Has something else happened?"

"Nothing big." She rubbed her forehead, as if trying to rub away a headache, and her voice sounded choked. "I just realized that the picture of my parents is missing. Someone took it."

He tried to make sense of that and couldn't. "Maybe you

put it someplace else. Or it fell on the floor and the maid put it away in the wrong place."

"No." She shook her head. "I know those are rational answers, but I don't believe them. Someone took it from my room—someone who can walk freely around this house."

"I'm sorry. I don't know what we can do about it now. Maybe tomorrow—"

"It's not that." A shiver ran through her. "It just made me realize how dangerous the situation is. Baxter's in there alone with just the nurse to protect him."

"And me." He forced a smile. "I won't let anyone get by me."

"I want to sit with him, just to be on the safe side." She reached for the doorknob again.

He grasped her hand, stopping its motion. "I can't let you do that."

"What?" For a moment she stared at him, blue eyes wide, as if she didn't understand what he'd said. Then recognition came flooding in. "You think I'd try to hurt him?" Her voice rose.

"Shh." He sent a warning glance toward the door. "It's not that."

"Then what is it? He's my grandfather, whether either of us likes it or not. I have a right to see that he's safe, no matter what you say."

He was making her hate him. He couldn't do anything else.

"I can't let you in. I said that no one would have access to him tonight, and that includes you."

Her lips trembled for just an instant before she pressed them into a firm line. "Then you do suspect me."

How could he deny it, when the faintest chance that he was wrong might mean Baxter's life?

"Don't you see that I'm protecting you as well as Baxter?" His fingers tightened on hers. Why couldn't she understand that he was trying to do his best for everyone? "If you went into his room and something happened to him tonight, no one would believe you didn't do it. I'm doing what's best for both of you."

She shook her head slowly, and the pain she felt seemed to surge through their clasped hands and pummel him in the heart. "You think I'm capable of murder." Her lips twisted. "Like Lydia. She thinks my mother was a murderer, so why shouldn't I be just like her?"

"Corrie, no!" How did he repair this and still do his duty by Baxter and the rest of the family?

She wrenched her hand free. "Don't bother, Lucas." All the color had left her face. "At least I know now where I stand with you."

Before he could say a word, she spun and hurried back to her room, closing the door sharply behind her.

By the next evening, Corrie was cried out. The pain in her heart hadn't lessened, but at least she no longer felt as if she'd double over with it.

The thought that there could ever be anything between her and Lucas had always been a futile one. She'd known that. She just hadn't realized that her foolish heart had continued to hope.

Well, that hope had been completely demolished, so she had to learn to live with that. She could do it—of course she could. But somehow she felt it would be a long time before her heart stopped grieving over Lucas.

She walked to her bedroom window and looked down at the garden. It had been another stormy afternoon, and although the rain had stopped, the clouds still hung low in the sky, bringing on an early dusk. The lights in the garden had come on, pale in the gloom. No one stirred.

She'd begun to feel like a ghost in the house. No one had spoken to her all day, and she certainly hadn't felt like seeking anyone out. Least of all Lucas—the pain freshened at the very thought of him.

She'd been aware of the doctor and nurses coming and going throughout the day. Baxter couldn't have awakened, or someone would have told her that.

And if he didn't? Or if he did and didn't remember how he'd gotten the overdose of medication? How long would it be before someone decided to bring the police into it? How long before the ugly thoughts became accusations?

I don't see my way any longer, Father. Please take my hand.

The telephone on the bedside table shrilled, startling her. A shiver went down her spine. She couldn't imagine that a call at this point would be good news.

She picked up the receiver. "Hello?"

"Corrie, thank goodness you're there." Lydia sounded frustrated, as if for once she'd come up against something she didn't know how to handle. "Will you come over to my place right away?"

"Why? What's wrong?" Her hand tightened convulsively on the receiver. *Bad news.*

"I'm watching Jason—Eulalie and Lucas both had to be out for a bit. I don't like the way his breathing sounds. He says you know what to do if he has an attack."

Her heart clenched. "Maybe I should get the nurse—"

"No, don't. She shouldn't leave Baxter." Her voice was unaccountably sharp. "He just wants you, for some reason."

Obviously Lydia couldn't imagine why.

"I'll be right there." She hung up, crossed the room quickly and trotted down the stairs.

The garden was as dark as it had looked from her window, the air motionless and heavy, as if someone had thrown a wet blanket over her. She hurried across the garden to Lydia's house, her mind busy with Jason. Would he have his inhaler with him? If not, would it be faster to go to Lucas's house for it or take him straight to the hospital?

Please, Father, be with Jason now. Calm him, and help me see the best thing to do.

Lydia was waiting when she reached the garden door. She ushered her in quickly, closing the door behind her. "He's right in there." She gestured toward the room that was a combination office and sitting room.

Corrie hurried around the edge of the leather couch, expecting to find Jason lying there. The couch was empty.

"Where is—" She turned toward Lydia as she spoke. The words died in her mouth.

Lydia's heavy gardening shovel swung in a deadly arc toward her head. She spun away. The blade struck her shoulder instead of her skull, sending pain stabbing down her arm, so intense that for an instant she couldn't breathe, couldn't think….

But she had to think. Lydia was coming at her again, shovel raised, her face as composed as if she chaired a committee meeting.

Corrie forced her legs to move. Stumble to the side, try to get out of the way of the blade, try to get to the door before it connected with her head.

She stumbled into the desk chair, sending a fresh, fierce slice of pain down her left arm. Useless, but her right arm still worked. She grabbed the wheeled chair and sent it rocketing toward Lydia. Lydia staggered backward, losing the shovel, arms windmilling.

Out, she had to get out while she could. She rushed toward the door, gasping a silent prayer. Almost there—

"Stop, Corrie." The voice was calm. "I don't want to have to shoot you."

She turned. Lydia held a small, deadly-looking gun in her hand.

There were no good options here. She edged another step toward the doorway. "You don't want to fire that thing. People will hear."

Lydia's smile flickered. "You'd be surprised at how often no one notices a gunshot. They think it's just a car backfiring."

Two more steps to the door. Should she risk it? Turn her back and run for it? The muscles in her back seemed to cringe in anticipation of the shot.

Lydia took a step to the side, moving the gun slightly. "Thinking of running? It's true I might miss you the way I did at the farm. But I couldn't miss him."

She gestured with the gun, and Corrie's heart stopped. Behind the armchair lay a small, huddled figure. Jason.

"No!" Corrie reached him in a few stumbling steps, dropping down and drawing him toward her. "What did you do to him?"

She looked up at Lydia. At the farm, she'd said. It had been Lydia. All those trophies of hers probably included some for shooting. This close, the gun no longer looked small. It looked enormous, capable of wiping her and Jason out of existence in a matter of seconds.

Jason. A surge of strength went through her as she cradled his limp body against her. She couldn't give up. She was Jason's only hope.

Lydia waved the gun as if the child were of no significance. "He's fine. I gave him a half of a sleeping pill, that's all. I just needed him to bring you here."

His breathing was shallow, but not rasping. Not yet. What would the effect of a sleeping pill be on an asthmatic child? Would it depress his breathing?

Please, Lord, please, Lord.

"Lydia, this is foolish." She had to sound calm, had to stay calm, for Jason's sake. "Whatever quarrel you think you have with me, you don't want to hurt a child."

"Quarrel?" Emotion surged into Lydia's face, turning it into a mask of rage, all the more startling because those were Lydia's calm, pleasant features. "You call it a quarrel?"

She struggled to think through the pain. The woman had clearly gone over the edge. She had to keep her talking, keep her from using that gun, until she could figure out what to do.

"I don't know what to call it. What have I ever done to you?"

The gun stopped wavering. The black hole pointed straight at her head.

"Don't be naive. You're trying to take what's mine, just like your mother did."

"My mother." Her mind stuttered, trying to find a firm point to clutch in a morass of confusion. "What does my mother have to do with this?"

"Your mother tried to take what was mine." Lydia's voice was eerily assured—her board chairman voice. "I had to take care of her. And now I have to take care of you."

* * *

Lucas sat next to Baxter's bed, hands clasped between his knees. Praying? He wasn't sure his mental ramblings consisted of prayers, but certainly he had a sense that he'd been trying to break through the long silences and hear God's will for his life again.

He'd hurt Corrie so badly. He hadn't intended to. He'd been trying to protect her as well as Baxter.

Somehow that excuse didn't bring him much comfort. He cared about Corrie, maybe even loved her, if he dared use that word. He should have trusted her.

She was only fifty feet or so away. He glanced at the door. He could go to her. Talk to her. Try to heal things between them. Didn't they both deserve that?

He braced his hands on the chair arms, pushing himself up, when a sound sent him turning toward the bed. Baxter groaned, then mumbled something, his head turning restlessly on the pillow.

The nurse started forward instantly, putting her hand on his pulse. "Mr. Manning? Can you hear me?"

Lucas leaned over her shoulder, willing Baxter to wake, willing him to end this nightmare. "Baxter, wake up. It's Lucas. I need to talk with you."

Baxter's face turned toward the sound of his voice. The nurse nodded. "Good. Keep talking to him."

"Come on, Baxter. Open your eyes." Open your eyes and tell us what happened to you.

His veined lids fluttered, and again his head moved restlessly on the pillow. "Can't," he murmured.

"Yes, you can." Lucas's voice was sharp, drawing a quick glance from the nurse. "Open your eyes."

With agonizing slowness, Baxter's eyes opened. For a

moment he seemed to stare at nothing, and then his gaze focused on Lucas's face.

"Lucas."

"That's right." He managed a smile. "You had us scared this time."

Baxter didn't respond to the smile. His head turned again, and his fingers twitched. "Can't think. Something I have to tell you."

He closed his hand over those frail, twitching fingers. "It's okay. Don't exert yourself. Just stay with us."

That earned a glare that almost made Baxter look like himself again. "What happened?"

He exchanged glances with the nurse, hers a warning. But Baxter had a right to know what had happened.

"It looks as if you had an overdose of medication. We're not sure how it happened."

Baxter's eyes fluttered closed. He frowned. Then his eyes opened again, staring, and his fingers grasped Lucas's.

"Corrie," he whispered. "Corrie."

He felt as if he'd been punched in his heart. It couldn't be. "Corrie?"

Baxter nodded, the effort to speak obviously exhausting him.

"Are you saying Corrie did this to you?"

"No. No." His hand fluttered. "Danger."

"Corrie's in danger how? From whom?" His heart was beating again, so fast it felt as if it would burst from his chest.

Baxter's eyes flickered closed again. He shook his arm. "Baxter, talk to me. Who threatens Corrie? Who did this?"

The nurse tried to pull him away from the bed. "Please, Mr. Santee. Let him rest."

He shook her off. "Not yet. Baxter, wake up. Tell me."

"Lydia." It was a bare whisper. "Lydia." He slumped down on the pillow, his breathing harsh.

The nurse elbowed him aside and bent over Baxter.

He took a step back. Lydia? That didn't make any sense. Lydia didn't have anything to gain by hurting Corrie. But if she'd done this to Baxter…

He spun, reaching the door in a few quick strides. Corrie. He had to check on her, make sure she stayed here, stayed safe, until Baxter woke again and they knew for sure.

He rapped on her bedroom door. No answer. He flung the door open. The bedside light was on, and her Bible lay facedown on the rumpled coverlet. It looked as if she'd gotten up in a hurry.

"Corrie!" he called sharply. No answer.

He took the steps two at a time, driven by an inner compulsion that had nothing to do with rational thought. At the bottom of the stairs he ran into Mrs. Andrews. She grasped his arm.

"What's happened? Is he worse?" Her round face crinkled with fear.

"He's better. Have you seen Corrie?"

"Oh, I'm so glad—"

His grip tightened on her arms. "Corrie. Have you seen her?"

Looking affronted, she pulled away from him. "Yes, certainly. Not long ago. I saw her going across the garden toward Miz Lydia's house."

Brushing past her, he raced for the back door and the wrought-iron steps that led down to the garden, his heart thudding in time with his feet.

Protect her, Father. His anguish broke through whatever barriers remained, shattering them. *Please, dear Lord, protect her. Let me be in time.*

SEVENTEEN

Corrie bent over Jason. Lydia had finally allowed her to move him to the couch, and it was all she could manage with only one good arm. Oddly enough, the pain seemed to be clearing her head, forcing her mind to intense concentration. If she and Jason were to survive this, she had to think, had to delay Lydia long enough for someone to come looking for Jason.

"He needs a doctor." She stroked his face with her good hand, glancing around under lowered lids for anything she could use as a weapon. "You know he has asthma. You never should have given him a sleeping pill."

"He'll be fine." Lydia smiled thinly. "He'll sleep through the whole thing, and everyone will think you ran away, just as they thought your mother ran away." She glanced toward the window, the gun never wavering. "We'll wait until it's a little darker, I think. It was after midnight when I took care of Gracie."

"You killed her."

"Of course." Lydia tilted her head, as if it were the most natural thing in the world. "She robbed me of Trey."

A spurt of anger went through her, totally separate from the fear. "You can't seriously think she pushed Trey."

"It was her fault he died." Her face darkened, and she took a step toward Corrie, hand seeming to tense on the gun. "I'd persuaded her that Trey was better off without her. She was going to go away. But when I told Trey, he reacted badly."

She saw the truth now, and it sickened her. "You pushed him."

"It was her fault." Lydia's voice rose. "He would have married me, if not for her." She seemed to hear the sound of her own voice and checked herself, her face smoothing out to its usual pleasant lines. "It will be fine. I took care of it before, and I will again."

"By killing me." She forced herself to say the words, hoping against hope Lydia would face what she was doing.

"Everything was fine until you came. I had my rightful place, living in Trey's house, being a part of the family. If you'd been a fraud, everything would have been all right. But you weren't, so I had to get rid of you."

Jason stirred, moaning a little. His eyelids flickered. Lydia motioned with the gun.

"Get up. We'll have to go now, before he wakes."

But it was too late. Jason blinked, opened his eyes, and stared at Lydia, seeing the gun. "What—what's happening?" Fear colored his voice. "Cousin Corrie?"

"It's all right, Jason." She had to keep her voice calm. "Don't be afraid."

"Jason will have to go along on our little boat ride, I think."

That was how she'd done it, of course. Lydia, handling that small boat of hers with such ease. No one would have thought anything about it, even if they'd seen her going out at night. Then she'd just had to drive Gracie's car to a Florida beach and send a scribbled postcard.

Jason, catching the menace in the air, gasped. His

breathing increased, and when he leaned against her she felt the rapid pounding of his heart. "Corrie—"

"Jason, it's okay." She tilted his head so that he focused on her, not Lydia. "Listen to me. You can stop this. You don't have to let it happen. Don't be scared. Just lean against me and take nice, slow breaths."

For an instant she thought he'd panic, but his gaze held hers, and he nodded slowly. She felt his struggle to control his breathing, felt his small body lean trustingly against her.

"Good boy. That's the way." She stroked his cheek. "That's my brave boy. You can do it."

He nodded, and she felt his breathing ease.

Show me, Father. I can't let her get Jason on that boat. I've got to stop her now.

The lamp on the side table had a nice, heavy pewter base. If she could grasp it quickly enough...

She leaned casually away from Jason, bringing herself a few inches closer to it. She'd have to twist to get it with her right hand. A small chance, but the only one she could see. If only something would distract Lydia, just for a moment or two.

Please, Lord.

The banging on the garden door came so quickly on her prayer that she almost couldn't believe it. Lydia craned to see who it was. The gun didn't waver, but the distraction let Corrie get precious inches closer to the lamp.

"Eulalie," Lydia muttered. "What's she doing back already?"

The crescendo of knocking increased, with Eulalie's voice added to the din. Lydia's hand sagged, just slightly, as she frowned in the direction of the door.

Now or never. Please, Father.

Corrie grasped the lamp and swept it toward Lydia's hand with all her might. The lamp crashed into her, striking her arm. Lydia cried out, but she didn't lose her grip on the gun. She turned it on Corrie, her finger tightened—

The window behind her shattered into fragments. Lucas burst through it. Corrie lunged toward the gun. Lydia struck at her, sending pain ricocheting down her arm. She couldn't hold on, she was losing her—

Then Lucas was there, grabbing Lydia and sending the gun spinning to the floor.

"I saw her through the window with the gun trained on Corrie and Jason." Lucas glanced toward his son, but Jason was sound asleep, leaning against Corrie's good arm. The whole family had gathered in Baxter's bedroom, trying to make sense of the unbelievable. "I knew I needed a distraction, and Eulalie did a wonderful job of that."

Baxter, propped up on his pillows, nodded. "Eulalie has the Manning nerve behind that soft exterior. I've always said that."

Corrie suspected he'd always said no such thing, but no one seemed inclined to argue the point.

Eulalie bridled. "The nerve of that woman. Taking my grandson that way. Thank the good Lord Corrie was there. If she hadn't thrown that lamp, I shudder to think what might have happened."

"Lucas would have handled her. He came through the window as if he'd been shot from a cannon."

Lucas smiled at her words. Maybe it would be better if he didn't know that smile turned her to marshmallow.

"You were all wonderful," Deidre said briskly. "Now tell

me how we're going to hush this up so all of Savannah isn't talking about us."

"I'm afraid there's no hushing it up," Lucas said, glancing at Baxter as if he expected an argument. "Lydia wouldn't shut up, even when the attorney I called for her told her to. She seemed to want everyone to know what she'd done."

"Mad as a hatter," Ainsley said. He put his arm around his mother's shoulders, as if he realized how close he'd come to losing her.

"That'll be up to the law to decide." Lucas glanced from one face to another. "We'd all better be prepared for the notoriety."

She waited for someone to point out that none of this would have happened if she hadn't come, but no one did.

"Let them talk." Baxter sounded as if he were ready for a fight. "Talk can't hurt us. Mannings are tougher than that." He tried to sit up straighter and then subsided with a gasp.

Eulalie bustled forward. "Now, that's just enough of that. Uncle Baxter, you need to rest. Everyone else can just clear out. We'll talk it all over in the morning."

Somewhat to Corrie's surprise, Baxter let her take control. The rest of them found themselves in the study, where Lucas put his sleeping son down gently on the sofa.

"Good night, Corrie." Ainsley gave her a quick kiss on the cheek. "Get some rest and don't worry about tomorrow."

Deidre didn't look inclined to kiss her, but she gave a quick nod. "We'll handle it together." She glanced at the sling cradling Corrie's broken left arm. "Do you need some help getting undressed?"

The offer touched her more than she'd have expected. "I'll be fine. Thank you. Both of you."

When he'd closed the door behind them, Lucas stood for a moment. "They're not such bad kids."

"I guess not." They were alone, and she didn't know what to expect. Had the revelations of the past few hours changed things between them? Or were they still caught in a web of past tragedies?

"Do you know what pushed her over the edge?" He covered the few steps between them.

She shook her head, her breath taken away by his sudden nearness.

"Baxter told her she'd have to vacate the house, because he was turning it over to you. She couldn't stand to give up that image she had of herself as Trey's widow. So she decided her only option was to get rid of you."

"The way she got rid of my parents."

He nodded. "She told the police all about it. How she struggled with Trey when he tried to go after Gracie. She says the fall was an accident, but I'm not sure I believe that."

A shiver went through her. "She thought she was rid of my mother, but when Gracie came back—"

"She had to have a fatal accident." The lines in his face deepened. "Lydia said she weighted her body down and dumped her at sea. Then she realized she had to do something with Gracie's car, so she drove it down to Jacksonville and sent that faked suicide note. Easy enough to rent a car to drive back. After all, no one knew Gracie had come except Eulalie, and she was too intimidated by Baxter to bring it up."

Corrie glanced toward the bedroom door. "She seems to be getting over being intimidated."

"Maybe Baxter has begun to realize how much he depends on her." Lucas shook his head. "I don't know why we're talking about Eulalie just now."

She couldn't quite manage to meet his eyes. "What do you want to talk about?"

"You." He took her hand in his, and she seemed to feel that touch in every nerve in her body. "I'm sorry, Corrie. About what happened to your mother, I mean. It's rough to find out in such a way."

She swallowed to ease the tightness in her throat. "Yes. But at least I know now that she didn't desert me. The last thing she did was come back to a place she had every reason to hate, just so she could make a better life for me."

"She was brave. Like you."

She shook her head. "I didn't feel very brave, but I wasn't going to go without a fight. Especially not after Jason woke up. I still can't believe she was prepared to hurt him."

Her voice broke on a little sob then. Lucas made some inarticulate sound and pulled her into his arms. His lips pressed against her hair. "You saved him."

"You saved both of us."

He leaned back so that he could see her face. "Maybe we'd better say that God saved all of us."

"Yes."

He touched her cheek, his fingertips feather-light. "Corrie, you know the worst of us now. We're a pretty eccentric bunch. Baxter may be a bit amenable for a while, since he's had a good scare. Maybe we'll be able to get him to see sense about the way he treats Ainsley and Deidre."

Her heart seemed to be beating up in her throat, so that she could hardly speak. "We?"

"We," he said softly. "I thought there was no hope for us, but I was wrong. What we have is strong enough to see us through, if you're willing to be part of such a crazy family."

"Seems as if I already am." Strength flooded through her. "Are you asking me to be your cousin, Lucas?"

He cradled her face between his hands, his touch tender. "I'm asking you to be my love, Corrie. Will you?"

"I came to Savannah to find out who I am and where I belong," she said carefully, wanting to spell it out. "I found out what I've always known—that I'm God's child. And I found out where I belong. With you."

His smile broke through, then. As he lowered his lips to hers, she thought again of the love in her parents' young faces. In spite of all the barriers between them, it had been real.

Thank You, she thought. *Thank You.*

* * * * *

Dear Reader,

I'm so glad you decided to pick up this book, the second in my Lowcountry romantic suspense series. Corrie's search for her true identity resonated with me, and I hope it will with you.

It's always a joy to go back to the lowcountry of the Georgia and South Carolina coast, the setting for my earlier Caldwell Kin series. It's a beautiful area, filled with mystery and romance as well as with friendly people who love to make you feel at home. Savannah, the setting for this story, is surely one of the loveliest, most unique cities in the country. Each time I'm there I find something I hadn't discovered before, and my affection for the city deepens.

I hope you'll write and let me know how you liked this story. Address your letter to me at Steeple Hill Books, 233 Broadway, Suite 1001, New York, NY 10279, and I'll be happy to send you a signed bookmark. You can visit me on the Web at www.martaperry.com or e-mail me at marta@martaperry.com.

Blessings,

Marta Perry

QUESTIONS FOR DISCUSSION

1. Corrie's situation is similar to that of many adopted children, who long to know about their birth parents. Have you ever known anyone in that situation? How do you feel about it?

2. Did you find yourself sympathetic to Corrie's longing to understand her parents? Would you have done the same in her place, or would you have been able to go on without knowing?

3. Corrie's Aunt Ella thinks she should be content with knowing that she is a child of God. Was Corrie content with that in the beginning of the story? How did her feelings change by the end of the story? Did they?

4. Lucas feels as if he carries the weight of responsibility for the whole extended family. Do you know anyone who has that sort of responsibility? Might it be difficult not to feel resentment over that burden at times?

5. Unable to trust these new relatives of hers, Corrie doesn't tell them everything. In turn, this makes them even more suspicious of her. How could they break through that suspicion?

6. Deidre and Ainsley both hide their activities because of Baxter's strictness. Do you find that a natural response? How did Baxter's ideas of what was best for them conflict with their longings and ambitions? Why do you suppose he didn't recognize that?

7. Do you think Lucas was overprotective in relation to his son's asthma? Why or why not? Could you understand his feelings? Have you experienced the difficulty of maintaining the right balance between protecting and coddling a child?

8. Even though she's attracted to Lucas, Corrie tells herself that her parents' example proves that mixing two such different worlds can only lead to tragedy. Do you think that's accurate? Do you know people who've made a success of marriage despite coming from very different backgrounds? How did they do it?

9. The scripture theme for this story is Psalms 139:15, printed at the front of this book. How do you feel that was reflected in Corrie's growth?

10. Does that passage provide comfort to you? Why or why not? Is there another verse which you feel better reflects your relationship to God? What is it and why is it meaningful to you?

And now turn the page for a sneak preview of
SEASON OF SECRETS,
the next Southern set romantic suspense
by RITA® award finalist Marta Perry.
On sale in October 2006
from Steeple Hill Books.

"Why is he coming back now?"

Aunt Kate put her morning cup of Earl Grey back in the saucer as she asked the question for what had to be the twentieth time since they'd heard the news, her faded blue eyes puckered with distress. December sunlight streamed through the lace curtains on the bay window in the breakfast room, casting sharp relief into the veins that stood out on her hand that was pressed to the polished tabletop.

"I don't know, dear."

Love swept through Dinah Westlake, obliterating her own fears about Marc Devlin's return to Charleston. She covered the trembling hand with her own, trying to infuse her great-aunt with her own warmth. Anger sparked. Marc shouldn't come back, upsetting their lives once again.

"Maybe he just wants to sell the house since the Farriers moved out." Aunt Kate sounded hopeful as she glanced toward the front window and the house that stood across the street in the quiet Charleston historic block.

Annabel's house. The house where Annabel died.

Dinah forced herself to focus on the question. "I suppose so. Do you know if he's bringing Court?"

Her cousin Annabel's son had been three when she'd

seen him last, and now he was thirteen. She remembered a soft, cuddly child who'd snuggled up next to her, begging for just one more bedtime story. It was unlikely that Courtney would want or need anything from her now.

"I don't know." Aunt Kate's lips firmed into a thin line. "I hope not."

Dinah blinked. "Don't you want to see Courtney?" This visit was the first indication that Marc would let his son have a relationship with his mother's kin that consisted of more than letters, gifts, and brief thank-you notes.

Tears threatened to spill over onto her great-aunt's soft cheeks. "Of course I do. But that poor child shouldn't be exposed to the house where his mother died, even if it means I never see him again."

"Aunt Kate—" Dinah's words died. She couldn't say anything that would make a difference because she understood only too well what her aunt felt. She, too, had not been back in that house since Annabel's funeral.

Except in the occasional nightmare. Then, she stood again on the graceful curving staircase of Annabel and Marc's house, looking down toward the dim hallway, hearing angry voices from the front parlor. Knowing something terrible was about to happen. Unable to prevent it.

"Everyone will start talking about Annabel's death again." Aunt Kate touched a lacy handkerchief to her eyes, unable as always to say the uglier word. *Murder.* "Just when it's forgotten, people will start to talk again."

Something recoiled in Dinah. It seemed so disloyal never to talk about Annabel. Still, if that was how Aunt Kate dealt with the pain, maybe it was better than having nightmares.

She slid her chair back, patting her aunt's hand. "Don't

worry about it too much, dear. I'm sure people are so busy getting ready for the Christmas holidays that Marc will have been and gone before anyone takes notice."

Her aunt clasped her hand firmly. "You're not going to the office today, are you? Dinah, you have to stay home. What if he comes?"

It was no use pointing out to her that Dinah was going to police headquarters, not an office. Aunt Kate couldn't possibly refer to her as a forensic scientist. In Aunt Kate's mind, a Charleston lady devoted herself to the church, charity and society—not necessarily in that order.

"I thought I'd check in this morning." As a freelance police artist she only worked when called on, but she'd found it helped her acceptance with the detectives to remind them of her presence now and then.

"Please, Dinah. Stay home today."

Her hesitation lasted only an instant. Aunt Kate had taken care of her. Now it was her turn. She bent to press her cheek against Aunt Kate's.

"Of course I will, if that's what you want. But given the way he's cut ties with us, I don't expect Marcus Devlin to show up on our doorstep any time soon."

Was she being a complete coward? Maybe so. But she'd fought her way back from the terror of the night Annabel died, and she had no desire to revisit that dreadful time.

Please, God. Please let me forget.

That was a petition that was hardly likely to be granted, now that Marc Devlin was coming home.

After helping her aunt to the sunroom that looked over her garden, where she would doze in the winter sunshine, Dinah cleared the breakfast dishes. It was one of the few things Alice Jones, her aunt's devoted housekeeper, allowed her to do to help.

Alice was nearly as old as her great-aunt, and the two of them couldn't hope to stay on in the elegant, inconvenient antebellum house on Tradd Street if she weren't here. She wasn't even sure when she'd gone from being the cosseted little girl of the house to being the caretaker, but she didn't see the situation changing any time soon and she wouldn't want it to.

A sound disturbed the morning quiet. Someone wielded the brass dolphin knocker on the front door with brisk energy. It could be anyone. Her stomach tightened; the back of her neck prickling. Instinct said it was Marc.

Heart thudding, she crossed the Oriental carpet that had covered the hall floor for a hundred years or so. She turned the brass knob and opened the door.

Instinct was right. Her cousin's husband stood on the covered veranda, hand arrested as he raised it to attack the knocker again. A shaft of winter sunlight, filtered through the branches of the magnolia tree, struck hair that was still glossy black.

For a moment Dinah could only stare. It was Marc, of course, but in another sense it wasn't. This wasn't the intent, idealistic young prosecutor her teenage dreams had idolized.

"Dinah." He spoke first, his deep voice breaking the spell that held her silent. "It's been a long time."

• • • • •